PATON

MIRIKA MAYO
CORNELIUS

author of Secret and Colored Lily, Poppa Took My
Innocence

PATON

PATON

This is a work of fiction. Names, characters, places and incidents are either products of the author's imagination or are used fictitiously. Any resemblance to actual events or locales or persons, living or dead, is entirely coincidental.

Free Picture: Old House ID: 198506
© Freds | Dreamstime Stock Photos

Woman in window illustration by Lawrence J. Mayo

mirikacornelius.com

PATON

<u>Acknowledgements</u>

All glory, honor, praise and total worship to God Almighty, Jesus Christ and Holy Spirit for every single thing because without Him, I am nothing.

To my son, I love you. To my husband as well, I love you. My parents – you rock, I love you, and thanks for everything. Although gone from earth but always present and alive with the Lord, my granny Dora, I love you still. See you and the rest when I get there.

To my readers, thank you and I want you to enjoy this one as you have enjoyed the others. Thanks for your support.

mirikacornelius.com

PATON

Table of Contents

PATON

PATON

The third and final book from the Secret & Colored Lily:
Poppa Took My Innocence novel series, also known as

The Secret Novel Collection

PATON

THE BOY

"Get down, man, get down!"

"Watch out, Paton, man. Move over," a tall and lanky teenage boy by the name of Jesse strained as he shoved himself against the bottom of the wall as a car passed by. "They gon' see me, Pate! I ain't got no room, man, I ain't got no room." The heel of his shoe dug into the dirt as his body scraped against the wall of jagged bricks, leaving patches of white dirt on his evenly toned, milky brown skin.

Paton, who was seated directly behind Jesse, lost his balance while crouched down and fell backwards, slamming the back of his head into the other teenager behind him who goes by the name of Drowning Boy, a nickname given to him as a result of him nearly drowning more times than any other person that ever set two feet in water. When Paton turned around, blood dripped from Drowning Boy's bottom lip, but he quickly put his finger up to his mouth, warning him not to make a sound.

"Shh…don't say nothing." Then, Paton carefully turned back to Jesse who had already stopped breathing altogether. Even when Paton touched him on the shoulder to get his attention, Jesse didn't move a muscle because the fear of being near death had already crept over him. Paton continued to whisper to him anyway, "You got to peek around the corner, Jesse, to see if those white men are still there."

"I ain't doing nothing," Jesse sharply retorted, finding it hard to inhale after the words escaped his mouth. He was so scared that he was trembling in the ninety-eight degree weather. "Ain't no way I'm peeking nowhere! That car full of white 'uns could'a stopped, and they might even be coming this way! We need to run, Pate, while we still got legs," he whispered while sweat dripped from his face onto his lips as the overpowering sun beamed directly into the entrance of the segregated restroom area that sat off on the side of the road.

"Where we gonna go, huh, Jesse? Tell me that! Now stick your eyeballs around that wall and tell us what you see. Hurry up in case we gotta fight." He stared both of his long time friends in the eyes like his dad has always taught him to do when he wanted respect. "Ain't y'all got some fight in you? You better 'cause if they catch us, they shole is gonna fight us, but they gonna do it 'til we dead," he explained, smiling because he'd done this plenty of times all by himself at other stops. The last couple of times, he convinced his buddies to tag along with him, and the fact that they could be caught at any minute had everyone but Paton on shaky ground. Paton was only pretending to be terrified to play a prank on the other two.

Leaning forward, Jesse cautiously placed the whole side of his face against the dirty brick and then scooted it to the edge. On the other side of the brick wall, he saw nothing but high weeds and an empty road which came as a relief to him because inside his left hand was the Whites Only sign that he'd just removed from the top of the door that only Caucasians entered.

"Ain't nobody out here," Jesse stated, letting out a deep breath. "They gone, Pate. They gone. Get this thing outta my hand." Jesse threw the sign onto the Colored side of the restroom, and Paton burst into laughter. Drowning

Boy followed suit, and all the laughter made Jesse feel like he had to prove himself, prove he wasn't scared at all.

"Come on, y'all, get up. We gotta finish switching these signs before somebody comes. Get up quick," the young, seventeen year old Paton told his friends as he shoved his body off of Drowning Boy and pushed Jesse out of the way. He leaped to the other side of the restroom while Drowning Boy brushed the dust from his good pair of jeans with one hand and wiped his bloody mouth with the other. Drowning Boy was a heavy set young man, just turned eighteen years old and seemed to be still growing, not up but out. That was because whatever he found during the day, he ate. Every summer, he would win the hog eating contest where everyone got together to see who could eat the most of the pig. The contest was just two weeks ago, and Drowning Boy took the crown again for the third straight year. Drowning Boy had never met his dad who died soon after his birth, but according to his mother and the other ladies in the town, he was the huskiest man they had ever seen, not fat, but husky with huge shoulders and a chest that felt like pure iron. It was never a guess where Drowning Boy got his size.

"Look what you did to my lip, Pate," he complained.

Paton turned back to face him as he elevated the Whites Only sign into position where there was once a Colored Only sign. "Look at what you did to my head," he chuckled back. "The front of your face has more muscles than the back of my skull, Drowning Boy. Stop cryin', and keep a look out."

"We could go to jail for this," Drowning Boy continued, slowly looking around at the street, his paranoia having already taken over from their close encounter.

"We could, but ain't these some stupid rules to go to jail for? Ain't nothing different about the bathrooms 'cept a black butt sits on one toilet and a white butt on another. Ain't that right, Jesse, man? Plus, all that comes out is the dirtiest of us all! We ain't no different 'cept at the skin and hair. The crap comes out the same - green or brown!" Paton laughed as he turned to Jesse for help. "Come on and shove this nail in. I can't get it on this side good."

"Move out the way, Pate," Jesse responded, shoving Paton's leg resulting in him falling off the crate he used for elevation. "And move this crate, too. Grow some and you wouldn't need my help." Jesse was the tallest yet the youngest of them all at the age of fifteen. "Learn somethin' 'sides running your mouth and talkin' big…" he said to Paton who was known by his friends as the loudest one with the most jokes, until he got serious, which was a rarity and only with an enemy. He would always find a way to leave and calm down before doing something regrettable with his rage which could be overwhelming. This was something that his mother taught him from the time he was a little child, and so far, he'd held on to his mother's teachings.

As Drowning Boy grabbed Paton's arm to help him up from the ground, Paton caught movement from the side of his eye across the street in the corn fields. Dusting himself off, he leaned in to tap Jesse calmly on the leg and spoke.

"Get a move on, man. Them corn fields out there don't move without the wind or something alive moving them. It's either a dog or somebody watching us, Jesse, man."

Jesse immediately dropped one end of the Whites Only sign, and the nail that he attempted to manually drill back into the hole with his fingers, fell to the ground. Terrified, he spun around and stared at the corn field as a daring Paton walked out front, being the boldest of the two friends. Even though the corn stalks stopped moving, he was still paranoid because he knew those corn fields like the back of his hand. He would always race through them from the age of seven all the way to ten and never got caught snatching corn to take back home to his parents' kitchen table while he told them that it was a friend who would give it to him. Therefore, when he looked over into the corn fields, he knew exactly what he was looking for, someone who looked like him or someone who looked the opposite.

As sweat dripped from Paton's neck to drench his white T-shirt, Jesse inched closer to him. That was when Drowning Boy pushed himself away from the brick wall. They all searched the thick corn fields with their eyes but saw nothing for one silent minute until white skin revealed itself from beyond the green.

"Run, y'all, run!" Paton shouted as he escaped to the right, crossing over in front of Drowning Boy, and Jesse parted to the left. They all headed as fast as their feet could carry them to the back of the small brick building, but instead of crouching down, they kept running through the large field of high weeds. "Jesse, run!" Paton called loudly as his feet pounded the ground and the weeds whipped his legs like the switches his dad would use all the way up until he was twelve years old to make him behave. Paton watched as Jesse ran swifter than he'd ever seen him run before, and when he looked back behind him, two white men were chasing, gaining on them fast. "Keep goin', Drownin' Boy! Run!" he hollered to Drowning Boy who was tailing him.

"Paton! Pate, I can't make it. They comin'!" Drowning Boy called back, and the tone of his voice sounded of sheer terror.

"Come on, Drownin' Boy! Pick your feet up," Paton shouted, struggling to breathe as he tried to motivate his slower friend as much as he could, but then there was a gunshot. Without the slightest hint of hesitation, Paton fell directly to the ground and continued to crawl forward in another direction, but when he didn't hear Drowning Boy's feet behind him, he flipped over only to shuffle himself back to a crouched position.

"Pate! Drownin' Boy!" The yells of Jesse, who had already reached the trees, rang desperation into Paton's ears as he continued to wait on any sign of Drowning Boy. Just when he was about to move back toward the place he was running from, he heard a faint cry that deafened the sound of the pounding from his chest. Right after that came a deathly moan, and Paton recognized the voice as his good friend Drowning Boy.

Quickly, he attempted to peer through the dense weeds and high grass, but when that failed, he got the courage to lift his eyes as high as they could go above the weeds to not be detected. There were those same two white men pulling Drowning Boy off of the ground, but when they did, Drowning Boy clutched both his fists together like he was holding a baseball bat. Before the white man holding the gun turned his head to duck, Drowning Boy knocked his jaw so hard that blood squirted from his mouth. Along with the gun that flew from his hand, the white man fell to the ground as Drowning Boy grabbed the front of his stomach.

"Get outta here! Run! They gon' kill us! Run!" Drowning Boy shouted with all his might, and Paton fell back into the towering weeds, shaken in disbelief and fear, all of which was overpowered by his desire to help his wounded friend. Quickly, Paton dove forward, only about fifteen feet away from the man who Drowning Boy punched. Then, he started to crawl forward in a life or death effort to find the gun in order to help his friend.

"This nigger just hit me in my damn mouth, Lou, and I'm bleedin'! Oh, you done did it now, boy. How you like this?"

Paton stopped crawling and dropped to his stomach as the echo of Drowning Boy's holler sent waves of severe anxiety through his body. Trying to remain quiet while lying flat, the pressure became too much to withhold as the desperation for his friend to remain alive broke through his vocal chords, "Drowning Boy!" The veins in Paton's neck protruded as he cried defenselessly on the ground, and the force of his anger caused him to rise up onto his feet to face the men who wanted Drowning Boy dead.

As soon as he stood, his heart pounding to the beat of rage more than fear, he heard the voice of Jesse calling from the woods again, but he didn't turn around as he came into direct eye contact with the white man who'd just punched Drowning Boy so hard in his stomach that he was hunched over onto the other white man's arm suffocating and choking on his own blood as it fell heavily from his mouth.

"So the other little nigger boy wants to fight, too, huh? Come on over here, boy. Don't you know whose land this 'longs to now? This here my cousin's land now. Bought and paid for yesterday, and he don't take too kindly to niggers such as yourselves coming through here no more."

"We ain't know nothing about that! We ain't know nothing about the sellin' of no land or this property. Let him go!" Paton's nostrils flared, and his eyes seemed to suffer from a lack of oxygen as they turned red while he memorized the man walking toward him. He was around five feet five inches tall with jet black, straight hair that went from the top

17

of his head to the thin of his chin. When the hair on his face reached the chin's narrowest part, there was a split – no hair at all. As Paton continued to study him, he didn't move as he watched the man lean over and pick up the gun that fell from his hands minutes ago. In Paton's mind, there was absolutely nothing that would make him leave Drowning Boy but death, so as long as he could see Drowning Boy alive, he was gonna stay with him, especially knowing in the back of his mind that none of them would have been in this position if it wasn't for him.

"What was y'all doing back there at them bathrooms that's sittin' on my family's property, boy? Them bathrooms so close to the field, hell, they may as well belong to us, too," he laughed. "Soon as you seen us, you took off running there," he continued as he pointed the gun directly at Paton's chest, but Paton didn't flinch.

"We wasn't doing nothing but fixing the sign. Ain't no law of death required for that."

"What sign? You looks guilty to me," the white man continued, swinging his gun from side to side with a huge ball of tobacco tucked in the side of his mouth. Then, he tilted his head back while his eyes stay planted on Paton and began speaking to the man holding Drowning Boy. "Hey, Lou, drop that big nigger on the ground and run back there to see if there's a sign that needs fixin'. This boy here says that they was just fixin' a sign, so I suppose there's one back there broken. Go check," he commanded as Paton stared down the barrel of his gun. "And you bet' not move an inch because if you're lyin', I'm gonna blow your head sky high," he threatened.

Paton turned his attention to his friend who was laying there on the ground gasping for air as his body dug into the dirt from him trying to handle the pain. The huge guy he had grown up with was now reduced to near death, and the only thing Paton could do was shout, "Drowning Boy, keep breathing. Keep breathin'!" Then, he turned to stare back into the eyes of the gunman, and the very threat of Paton's anger burst through his skin, so much so that the white man with the gun reminded him of his earlier threat.

"You jump, and I'll kill you, boy. You jump, and I'll shoot you dead. Be laying here with your bastard friend here. Ain't that, right? Ain't all y'all black bastards there, boy? You even much got a last name?" he taunted, growing extra courage from his gun as Paton's anger grew worse, and his breathing deepened as his eyes gravitated toward the trigger. His hands grew extremely light, just like a feather, as he motivated himself to fight as well as kill if he had to do so. The blood continued to drip lightly from where Drowning Boy punched the white man in the mouth, and each time it dripped, Paton became distracted, hearing his mother in the back of his mind, warning him to calm down.

"Whatcha' thinkin' 'bout, boy? You want this here gun?" With his hairy arms, the white man leaned over and practically handed him the gun in a provoking manner. "Go ahead, Pate. Ain't that your name? Pate? Or is it Nate...or Late...or Mate? Hell, boy, y'all can't spell nor speak, ain't that right? Where's your other friend?" he asked, aiming the gun in the direction of the woods. "You think he still back there, boy? I tell you what," he continued, walking in closer to Paton, so close that Paton could smell his dirty breath. "When I find him, I'ma kill him, too, if you lying about that sign back there. Ain't got to be no law against nothing. I make my own law 'gainst niggers."

"The sign was off, and when we saw you in the corn, we got scared and ran. We was just using the bathroom," Paton gritted his teeth as the words passed through his lips. "And it ain't nothing but a sign!" he finally shouted, trembling in the hot sun. "It's just a sign! That's a human bein'! He just like you 'cept a different color! Go shoot them men that burn them crosses and…" he paused, gathering his breath before speaking again. "It's just a sign," he stated, hopelessly thinking about how that sign meant more to them being that they were white than it did to him. "I just want my friend, so we can get him some help. He needs some…"

"Hey, Tommy!" called the other man on the way back from the bathroom. "Yeah, that sign there is hanging off. I put it back up on there. Looks like the boys were telling the truth. You can let 'em go."

"Well, hey!" Tommy spun around to face his fellow lyncher. "I guess we got into a fight with these boys here for nothing. Hey, boy! You can go home now," he hollered down at Drowning Boy who was only taking minute breaths. "Whatcha' waitin' on?" he questioned, staring back at Paton. "Come get your friend before he die out here on my cousin's land. Nigger blood'll make the crops die, won't it, Lou?"

"Something like that, Tommy," he grinned, walking quickly back to where Drowning Boy laid.

"You ain't have to shoot him," Paton stormed past the man with the gun, and when he reached Drowning Boy, he lifted him, using all the strength he could muster. Drowning Boy stumbled heavily onto Paton's body, nearly causing him to fall backwards, but Paton stood strong as both white men stood back and grinned as he struggled. "You're gonna have to walk, DB. I got to get you some help," he strained as tears started to flow from his eyes at the sight of what looked to him like pools of blood coming from Drowning Boy's belly.

"Oh, he'll be alright. Get that big boy on home, and put him in the tub. Wash him down. Be fine in the morning.

I done seen niggers that size climb down from a rope 'round their necks, so a bullet ain't went that deep. Come on, Lou," he called at his friend, but turns back to warn Paton. "If you come back through here, any of you, I'll kill all three of you. Walk the road. This here is family property now. No more short cuts. We got rights, and we shoot to kill."

Paton didn't stick around to listen to a menial word coming from the man's mouth. Instead, he was consumed with dragging his bloody friend along with all the strength and stamina he could muster while calling Jesse's name at the top of his lungs. He knew for a fact that Jesse was somewhere still around watching. "Jesse! Come back. I need you back here for Drownin' Boy. Jesse, he dyin'! They let us go, so come on back." Paton turned back and watched the two white men walking away, and then he shouted into the woods again. "Jesse, they leavin'! Come on, or Drownin' Boy ain't gonna make it." He ain't!"

Sweat drenched Paton's shirt as it mixed with the blood of his vulnerable friend, only to turn his white shirt red as Drowning Boy gripped tightly to the shirt's bottom. Drowning Boy's weight became too much for Paton to handle, resulting in him pounding into the ground with his knees as Drowning Boy fell to his side. That was when Paton spotted Jesse running back towards them, his eyes larger than they'd ever been because he was struck with pure fear. Once again, Paton took a deep breath to help Drowning Boy back onto his feet..

"Stand him up, Jesse, stand him up. Grab his legs and bend 'em. You can do it, come on, DB. Come on!" he yelled, but the more he tried to force Drowning Boy, the worse the situation got.

"We gotta drag him, Pate. Let's drag him...by his legs. You get one, and I get one. Keep him on his back. We get him to the woods, outta this sun and off this land, and then I go for help. Get him off this land 'fore them men come back out here and do what they did to him to us."

"Let's go," Paton responded. "Get the left one, and I'll take the right. Now pull. We ain't got no time to think about them and what they claim they gonna do to us. Got no time for it, so pull."

As they pulled, Drowning Boy's body was rescued from being cut by the many rocks in the soil because the weeds fell underneath him providing a sheeted cushion. Drowning Boy's eyes ended up shifting permanently from white and brown to bloodshot as he started to choke on his own blood. Therefore, when his body reached the edge of the woods, Paton flipped him over onto his side.

"Jesse, run and go get some help. Hurry up 'cause I don't know if he's gonna make it." As Jesse set off with the speed of lightening through the woods, Paton erupted into desperate pleas for help as loudly as he could as his voice cracked through the screams. "Help! Somebody, help us! It's Drowning Boy!" As he peered back into the eyes of the wounded, he ripped his own shirt off and began to wipe the blood from inside of Drowning Boy's mouth. The blood came out extremely thick on the shirt until he had to wipe it off on his pants and try again.

Drowning Boy tried to talk, but each time he took a shallow breath, no sound escaped. That's when Paton rushed behind him and lifted his upper body from the ground so that he could be in a seated position, but that caused his head to drop forward. This created even more of a panic inside of Paton, so he leaned him back into his arms, continuing to shake him to keep him alive. The woods closed in on Paton as he sat there, tired of desperately yelling for help and crying the hardest he'd ever cried. The end of his hope came when he finally looked back into Drowning Boys eyes. They weren't looking back, but only staring into the clear, blue sky.

Paton's stomach quaked as a loud groan traveled from the deepest part of his soul to the outside of his body as he held a dead Drowning Boy in his arms. With his forearm, he wiped all the blood from Drowning Boy's face, attempting to get it as clean as possible while his tears drenched Drowning Boy's face. "I'm sorry," he choked on his words as the sorrow overtook him. "It was just a stupid sign," he continued as he rocked back and forth, squeezing Drowning Boy at his chest as he recalled how he convinced both Drowning Boy and Jesse to come along with him as he pulled the prank. He'd done it plenty times before, and although he knew he would get in trouble if he ever got caught, he never thought it would cost a life - his or anyone else's. To him, it was just a silly prank.

"I didn't mean it, DB, I didn't mean it. I was just foolin' 'round, just foolin' 'round, so go ahead and wake back up. They gone now, look and see for yourself," Paton struggled to turn Drowning Boy's body to face behind them for the two white men who shot him, but they were long gone. His friend's head only rested on his chest, continuing to stare into the sky. Finally, he heard Jesse far off alerting him to his arrival, but things changed for Paton. His legs and arms began to shake like it was a cold day in the middle of winter. His tears stopped coming, and he went into shock, having a mental breakdown. Paton noticed the people coming toward him, following Jesse, but he didn't move. Instead, he began to speak rather calmly, as if nothing had happened.

"We're over here, just sittin' down." Still holding on to Drowning Boy, Paton continued rambling as Jesse was the first person to reach him.

"Paton, come on, man. Help us get him up," he said urgently while he examined his friend who was having a fit of grins, and Jesse didn't understand why. "Paton?" he asked, leaning his skinny body forward, but almost immediately, Paton's state frightened him, causing him to back away.

"Yeah, I'm trying to get him up, but he won't move," he laughed as he responded to Jesse. "I guess he caught himself pinning me down. You know how he likes to prove he stronger than me…and you."

As two other men and a woman approached the scene, Jesse stopped one of the men and pointed down at Paton. "Something's wrong with him…Paton…the one right there holding Drowning Boy. He ain't acting right. He ain't right, mister," Jesse complained while he stared, terrified at Paton's demeanor because he was shaking with laughter as his eyes were big and bright as the days of summer.

"That's Drowning Boy! Oh dear God on my soul, that's Ethel's baby," the woman cried as she stepped over into the weeds to get a better look at the dying boy as her long dress dragged the dirty ground. She leaned over slowly with her hand against her chest and made sure the young man fighting for his life was who she thought he was. When she was satisfied with her identification of the wounded boy, she rushed off back through the woods quickly, thoroughly upset and praying.

One of the men cautiously approached Paton on the left while the other moved to Paton's right side as Jesse backed further up, all of them prepared to separate Drowning Boy from an unstable and emotionally exhausted Paton. Because of how tightly Paton held on to Drowning Boy's chest and how he was grinning through his tears, it was obvious that something had gone wrong inside his head.

"Listen to me now, son. It's time," started the unknown man whose arms are covered in welts from running through the trees carelessly, "to let us help you with…"

"Drowning Boy…his name is Drowning Boy, William is the real name, though," Jesse interrupted. The man quickly lifted his finger up at Jesse who fell silent immediately but still waving his hand to try and force Paton to snap out of his trance.

"Look here, son. I've heard a lot about your friend here, and this is the first time I'm meeting him." He looked down at the top of Drowning Boy's lowered and lifeless head. "I'm Mister Himes." He introduced himself while glancing around him to be sure that the area was safe, and then he looked back at Paton. "Me and my friend here are gonna help you get up with Drowning Boy so we can get off this here land 'fore sundown. Things not looking too well 'round here, son. Don't know the folks here no more, so it's better we stick to our side for a while."

"Well, that's good you're here 'cause we been down here for a mighty long time, Mister Himes. I think we stuck," he laughed, continuing to squeeze Drowning Boy tightly, like his own life depended on them staying together.

"Reach out your hand to me, son, so I can get you up first. This'll be a real hard move if'n you stay close to him like you is…"

"I told you we stuck!" Paton shouted, creating a disturbance so great that and both men move back a couple of steps, confused as to why Paton accepted the help but declined it only seconds later. "There was a bullet that went down there in his gut," he continued, pointing with his chin down at the area where Drowning Boy was shot. "Y'all see that? I'ma stay here with him until he all better is all," he cried, the tears unloading onto his bare chest. "I'm staying right here 'til he heals up. Y'all welcome to sit…here…" He removed one of his arms from around Drowning Boy to clear off an area beside him on the ground, shoving the rocks away in order to make a smooth seat for anyone who wanted to join them. While Paton was distracted making a seat for the others, the two men who came to Drowning Boy's aid grabbed both Paton's arms, forcefully pulling him away from Drowning Boy. Just as fast as they did that, one of the men caught Drowning Boy's body before it hit the ground.

"Get off'a me! Get off!" Paton fought with a strength so tremendous that Jesse had to leap over Drowning Boy and help contain Paton so that they could get Drowning Boy some help faster.

"Get his legs off the ground, Jesse, because I got to pin him so you can go get more help. I don't wanna hurt the boy, so when he kicks again, grab his leg, so I can put him down," he ordered, battling with a mindlessly mad Paton. Jesse shuffled to the front of Paton, and as soon as his foot lifted from the ground, Jesse took hold of it, lifted it high, and the man put Paton down stomach first into the dirt with his arm behind his back. "Now go on and get some more help. Y'all friend is dead now, so go and get both they parents, mainly this boy here daddy if'n ya can, and then get the folks of the dead one."

"This boy that done been shot to death ain't got no daddy, Himes," the other man interjected. "Look just like his deceased daddy, though. Big as an ox. He's the only child from his momma. It's gone' kill her, you hear me, Himes? It's gone shole kill her to see her son done gone and left here." He placed Drowning Boy's dead body on the ground, removed his shirt and with it, cleaned him off the best way he could. All it did was smear the blood. "I'ma run on near the creek to get some water to wipe him down some."

26

PATON

"Go 'head. We can't lift him 'cause of this boy here under me. Gone then, before his momma see him. The creek ain't to far off. It's just right up the way."

As Mister Himes watched him rush away, Paton continued to struggle underneath him, gasping for breath and choking from the amount of dust getting chalked up into his mouth. Beginning to cough violently, he felt some pressure relieved off of his back by Mister Himes, and he was able to inhale better. Mister Himes then began to tell him a story.

"I used to be your age one time, and everything looked so fresh and new there, son. Ain't nothing seem the matter with nothin', but as time goes on, something seems the matter with everything 'round you. I was a youngster when my own poppa got killed by some white men out yonder 'round 'bout fifty somethin' odd miles from this spot. They killed him right there in front of me and my momma for nothing. They shole did. We was walking from the store after he finally got the money up to get some food for the kitchen. Well, poppa used to say that he would protect us with his life, and he did that, that day there sho'nuff. We still had about two hours to get outta that area 'fore darkness catch us, but it looked like them white men didn't want us there at anytime. That was the only way to get to our house though, lessen we crossed the water. I was too short at that time being I was just a boy to cross some deep water like that. When my daddy tried to explain and show them his watch for the time, they told him it was too late. That was a lie. Then, they say to him *"niggers can't tell no time"*, and then they hit him in the face for what they call back talk, or tryin' to correct them. My ma grabs me and runs off. They let us, and she was only doing what my daddy'd done told her to do if we ever ran into trouble. She was to get me to safety. Long story short, that's when I turned around and called my poppa only to watch him fall to the ground dead. Momma kept on running, and I did, too. I had to 'cause she

27

was dragging me. She told me to not regret what we did because we can't change it. Onliest thing to do now is to live. That's what I'm tellin' you, Paton. Live now, son. That's the only choice you got. Ain't nothing you coulda' done to change this here. Not nothin'. Let God take care of Drowning Boy now, and don't you go crazy here, son. You gon' make it like I did. Don't give the devil your mind, son, not like them people who shot ya' friend there. It'll kill you. It'll kill you faster than a bullet. You'll just be walkin' around dead, that's all. Just walkin' around here dead." He paused to place more of his weight on top of Paton. "Stop fightin' me, son. Stop fightin'. You look a lil bit like John Lee boy. You kin to him?"

Paton's struggle remained ongoing, refusing to listen while tensing up in a nonstop war of his strength against Mister Himes' strength, but Mister Himes held him down, halting his conversation because he could see that it wasn't working. As Paton laid there on the ground, the man who went to the creek came walking back toward the deceased with a soaked shirt in his hand. When he finally reached Drowning Boy, he wringed the water out so that it ran down the young man's face. Then, he wiped the blood from his skin.

"There we go," he sighed quietly, gathering the strength to say a prayer. "Father God in the name of Jesus, please keep his soul and let him fly, hold him in your arms, dear Lord, by and by. His rest came soon, but it didn't come sweet. Even so dear Lord, oh my God, it's Your face He will meet."

"Amen," said Mister Himes after his friend, James Lloyd, concluded the prayer. "Get that blood over there, James, by the boy ear there. I hear some people coming up now...you hear that?"

Paton's resistant demeanor changed in the blink of an eye after final resting words were prayed over Drowning Boy. His anger melted down into a lonely sorrow, so deep that he no longer wanted to live on the face of the earth again. With his face resting firmly in the dust and weeds, he watched as the man wiped the blood from Drowning Boy's face. He stopped breathing for about ten seconds when he finally noticed that Drowning Boy never moved a muscle. He was dead, and Paton finally accepted it.

"Yeah," he answered, reaching over to the other ear to catch the blood that was streaming down the side of Drowning Boy's face. "I hear 'em coming. I heard them on the way over here, and hopefully, we got plenty help with this because it ain't nothin' nice, Himes. This ain't nothing nice," he continued. "I hope they brings us a sheet…"

Right as he spoke, Paton's eyes turned downward to spot a man stomping fast through the trees, and following him came another one. Jesse was nowhere to be found. Both the oncoming men appeared horrified before they even got within fifteen feet of the body. Their eyes were wide open, and one of them even toted a gun in his hand as they came to a complete halt at the sight of Drowning Boy.

"We got us a wagon at the road on the other side, so we can lift him now. The boy named Jesse filled us in on what done happened here… and about that youngun' you sittin' on right yonder. Can you handle that one?" he asked referring to Paton who was now quiet while still pinned underneath Mister Himes.

"Yeah, yeah, I got him. He gonna be alright in time. Just need somebody to hold on to right now until his mind come back to him is all. Go 'head and lift him up, James. One of y'all take the middle and the other one take the legs so the weight is evened out. Thank y'all for coming now," he nodded to the unknown men as he pulled Paton up from the ground at the same time they lifted Drowning Boy.

Dirt was matted to Paton's face as he was lifted from the ground, but his eyes remained planted on Drowning Boy. Most of his strength was gone, but he gave one last try to resist the control of Mister Himes. It didn't work. Mister Himes was a brick laying man, and his muscles were fully matured in comparison to the young muscles of a growing Paton.

"Let's go, son. It's alright," Mister Himes consoled him as the others walked behind them through the naturally made path in the woods. Paton strained to look back as he walked forward, leaning on Mister Himes. During the short journey, he started to mumble to himself, and the words couldn't be made out by anyone – not even Mister Himes who walked right beside him. Paton sounded like the pure devil had taken over his body, and all he could do was fight to get his mind back. When they approached the edge of the street, a woman came dashing down the dirt road in a long skirt with no shoes on her feet, her hair freshly done, as if she just took out some rollers. In all her running, she didn't seem to feel the hard pebbles beneath her feet as she screamed deeply for whom everyone knew was her son. It was the widow Mrs. Ethel Washington.

"Willie! William!" her voice carried as she shoved the crowd of people out of her way so that she could get to the woods faster. A woman jumped in front of her in efforts to calm her down, but before the woman got two words from her mouth, William's mother knocked her to the ground with a slap so big that it froze everyone looking. Mrs. Washington jumped right over the woman she'd knocked over, and no one else dared try to stop her. She ran directly into the woods, and Paton's eyes stalked her every step, leaving him gasping for another breath when she dropped her body directly on top of her son, causing the men to lower him to the ground.

"Oh God, my baby," she wept loudly, "Please don't take him from me, Lord, please bring him back down here…I can't live no mo', Lord!" Her head pressed against her son's chest as she desperately stared into his face for a sign that God had put life back into his body if only for one moment. Then, she rubbed her hand down to his stomach where she felt the bullet's exit wound and released a deathly call that could disturb the dead. The moan was so deep and powerful that if people could see angels in the sky, they would have all been staring down at her. For minutes, she called for God Almighty to bring him back, but then ceased.

"Who shot my son?" she asked quietly, but when she got no answer, she demanded one with her voice. "I said, who shot my son? He's my only boy…my only boy… now somebody is gon' tell me who shot him so's I can kill him today!" She turned her body around to stare at everyone in the crowd that had gathered to see what had become the worst spectacle in years and continued to petition everyone for answers. When her eyes met Paton's, his eyes fell to the ground, and Mister Himes tried his best to prevent him from shaking worse than what he already was. Paton's mouth began to open to answer Drowning Boy's mama's question, but he was suddenly forced to turn around. Mister Himes covered his mouth to prevent him from answering, and Mrs. Ethel Washington looked away. "And I don't care who it is! I want that white man's name, and I want him dead by mornin'." Then, she turned back to scold Paton with her eyes, but Paton didn't see her. He could only feel her walking closer to him, repeating the words she stated over again, digging for an answer so that she could take matters into her own hands. "You hear me? I wants him dead." She then turned back to face the woods. "You hear! I want you dead by mornin', even if it got to be by my own two hands. I curse you that every child you have born comes to death in a worse way that you did mine! I curse you to hell, and I'm gonna send you there, if'n I got to drag you down to the pits of fire and torment myself."

When she turned back around, tears drowned her face, and she moved slowly to her son who is laid on the ground. With the cleanest parts of her dress, she wiped the blood from his stomach and kissed his cheeks, each time pressing her lips against them for at least five to ten seconds as she breathed the scent of her son before it left forever. "Lord," she finally spoke again as everyone had their heads bowed at the call of the Almighty God, "If this ain't the last breath my son will take, let him come back to me now." She choked on her words, but continued, "But if this is the last of my son on earth with me, oh Jesus!" she screamed, clinching her fists together as the veins rise in her neck, arms and hands, "Then, Lord, give me strength as You rock him in Your arms 'til I sees him again. I want to come soon, Lord, please let me come see my boy soon…" she pleaded to God, her wails forming quakes that would uproot the trees.

Just then, Paton felt his first escape since Drowning Boy was shot dead behind him in the fields. There was another voice that came from the back of the somber crowd. The woman approaching was out of breath, and her feet scraped the ground because she barely had any energy left to lift her legs. In front of her was a man who walked silently yet strong and unafraid, without a hint of expression to his hardened face, and he seemed to no longer be aware that the woman behind him, his wife, was about five months into her pregnancy. His eyes were set on one person, and that was his son whom he saw mumbling and crying; his eyes bloodshot and his gaze coming from a source of confusion and despair. When Paton saw his mother grabbing her stomach and panting heavily, his mumbling silenced, and when he became aware of the stern appearance of his father, he stopped breathing altogether.

"It's alright, son. That there's your daddy. I thought that was your daddy because you looks just like him," he stated quietly to Paton as he began to quake harder than when he had his arms wrapped around Drowning Boy. Mister Himes stood taller, and as John Lee approached, he greeted him with the horrible news while some of the female onlookers took hold of his wife, Sarah, who was doubled over in pain. "John Lee, I been watchin' over your son here for a spell now. He ain't right in the head about now after his friend there been shot down cold in front of him," he explained pointing to Drowning Boy who was still covered by his mother's body as she heavily wept. "Found him there…wouldn't let his friend go, so I had to wrestle him to the ground. No harm done, though. He was talkin' out his head, so he needs…"

"Paton," John Lee stated with a demanding voice, interrupting Mister Himes in mid-sentence. When Paton continued to stare off into the distance at his mother, as if he yearned for her, John Lee stepped into his line of vision. "I'm not gone call you twice. Look me in my eyes," he ordered. Even though he wasn't shouting, the vibes from his voice display a rage that only Paton understands but others feel. Paton knew that his father was about to break, and he would kill for his family with no hesitation. If Paton didn't snap out of his distress, the next move would have been to go find the man with the gun, and Paton didn't want his father to die. "That there's over now," he continued as Paton stared back into his father's eyes, wanting to ask him for help but afraid of what would happen next. The one thing Paton's father never allowed was weakness from anything or anyone.

As soon as those words parted from John Lee's mouth, Drowning Boy's mom immediately looked back at him with hopelessness in her eyes and then screamed to the heavens again as she grabbed her son's neck. John Lee then continued, "Fix yourself and walk on home. Let's go. Ain't no whites 'fixina break you. You don't come this way no mo'." John Lee's eyes moved across the crowd of people and then back at Drowning Boy who laid dead in his mom's arms. "Respects." He tipped his head and stood Paton up straight with only the force of his eyes. Paton followed behind his father, each step awkward by his tremors. John Lee never touched him.

"We was changing the signs, pops. We was changing the signs, and," Paton started speaking in his gait, but when his father heard him confessing to what he'd done, he quickly turned around, rushed back to him and grabbed him by the shoulders.

"Changin' signs? Is that what you think, boy? Drownin' Boy got shot for changin' some signs 'round? Y'all was runnin'! Wasn't no attack there. Jesse done told me he heard the man, son. He heard him say to you...what was y'all doing over yonder?" He pointed in the direction of the incident. "Them white men ain't care 'bout no signs in this here reality. They's cared about killing some colored folk who been on that land! Ain't you think they coulda' just caught you and asked you somethin' and sent you on home? He shot him in the back. They asked about them signs after that, didn't they? Didn't they?" Paton's father shouted at him again, and Paton jolted an answer.

"Yes...yessir," he quivered, glancing up at the people who gawked his way, awaiting any response just like his father.

"Now straighten up! They was gone kill one of you anyway...them the new people in town. Them the Carvers, and they ain't never been friendly no time I been living to no

Coloreds. They only needed something to blame killin' you on. Don't go round yonder no mo'…" he paused, "Because I know the only reason they left you living is so you could tell the tale of 'em. Don't talk 'bout this no mo'." Paton glanced around at everyone, and spoke one last time before setting off on his trek back home with his son. "Let them folks die. They may be back, but let them die with the fear they try to cause. Stay from 'round 'em."

The only people who knew what and who Paton's father was talking about were those his age. Paton watched as Jesse walked over to someone to start asking questions while the rest of the children outside at the time, started tugging on their parents' clothes. They were all hushed. Some were carried off, and others left on their own, terrified at seeing Drowning Boy dead on the ground.

The crowd dispersed as Paton and his father walk by, some of the women holding their clasped hands up underneath their chins while shaking their heads. John Lee stood tall, stomping the ground like he could move it into an earthquake while he searched out his pregnant wife. Paton noticed that he didn't see his mom either, and he continued to look to the left and right, yearning for her comfort but couldn't find her. He scanned the crowd again, but saw her nowhere. Before he could even ask, one of the ladies runs from a nearby home.

"John Lee, wait!" she hollered as she limped over. "She's having that baby!" Out of breath, the woman dropped her hands down to her knees in order to hold herself up as she caught her breath. Even though she hadn't walked that far, it was as if she'd run miles the way her breath left her. "Come on, John Lee, hurry. Something's going wrong I tell ya'! Ain't nobody baby s'pose to come this early. We got to hurry now!"

Paton's heartbeat escalated and pounded so heavily like it was about to come straight out of his chest and leave a wound so great that no amount of consoling could repair. His father began to run toward the house from where the lady came, and Paton followed closely behind. His mind was in an even worse state of confusion as he realized Drowning Boy's blood still covered his hands and shirt. When he reached the top of the porch, at first he could see nothing because his father stood directly in front of him. Suddenly, however, the man who taught him to stand strong all his life and let nothing destroy him, fell to his knees and began to call out for his wife Sarah. Then, the entire bloody scene entered Paton's vision as he watched the man he knew as undefeatable, crawl defeated toward his wife who laid there with wet rags all over her head and blood pouring from her body. There was blood everywhere.

Paton watched spellbound as a woman threw a thin sheet on top of his mom who laid there passed out, and there was so much blood that it immediately began to come through. Although Sarah wasn't moving, sweat poured from her forehead like steam from boiling water in a pot because of the temperature inside the home. There was a pot of boiled water on the floor while the ladies continued to wipe her down and tried to drag John Lee away from his wife, but he wasn't going anywhere. Paton, then, hesitantly walked over closer to his mom and called her name.

"Mama," he stated quietly and then a second time more firm. "Mama." Tears rolled down his face as he watched his father moan and rock back and forth. He was holding something in his hands, and as Paton walked even closer, a woman grabbed him by his hand. He viciously shook her off and immediately his eyes fell on what looked like a half formed baby in his father's hands. Paton stumbled back against the wall and began to cringe as he stared back at his mom who, in his mind at that moment, wasn't only passed out, but dead.

"Mama! Don't die, Mama!" he reached out to grab her head, and two women fell on top of him, rushing to explain that they were doing all they could to keep her alive, but he didn't hear anything they said. All he saw was his mom, dad and a dead baby until he finally blacked out. Paton's head fell against the wooden floor while the blood trickled from his mom down the floor's wood grain.

***

"Paton…Paton," Janie, his sister, called for him as he rested inside his bed. "Paton, don't get up from the bed. I'm just needin' you to wake up some 'cause I gotta go take care of Ma and get dinner cooking. Here some of your clothes you need to go 'head and put up, fold 'em first because you know I don't like to iron no clothes," she complained as she held his shirts on her left arm and tapped him with her right hand.

"Well, what is it? Get up or stay sleep?" Paton moaned. Every time Paton opened his eyes, the only things he saw were his mom and his deceased sibling along with his dead best friend, Drowning Boy. Therefore, he remained asleep for most of the days since the deaths.

"It's both of 'em. Hurry up 'cause I have to take care of mom. She needs some beet juice real bad. She weak still since she lost all that blood, and I gotta make the collards and liver. Daddy spent his last quarters on that liver, and I got to go down to the garden so I can pick some more greens 'fore tomorrow."

Wiping his eyes, Paton sat up in the bed. He'd been asleep with a raggedy T-shirt on and cut off pants he made into shorts for the heat of the summer. The pants were already too short for him since he had a growth spurt, so since there was no such thing as throwing clothes out, he made the best of them.

"I'm gettin' up," he complained. His eyes were red as fire, and Janie noticed how the skin around his eyes bulged revealing the fact that he'd been crying much of the night. Paton had been trying to hide his pain by staying asleep or staying away from everyone for one whole week, and it had been only two days since Drowning Boy's funeral which was done quickly after his mom cleaned him up and laid him on the couch for the viewing. After that, the men up town made Drowning Boy a nice wooden coffin. A regular size coffin didn't look like his body would fit inside, so they expanded one. Although Paton and the rest of the family went to the funeral along with most of the town, Paton kept his head down nearly the whole time. The only time he looked up was when people passed by him to either shake his hand or give him a warm hug. The first thing Paton saw at the funeral was when they lowered Drowning Boy into the hole right next to his father's grave. Drowning Boy's mom tried to jump over into the ground with him when his coffin got settled down in there. As a matter of fact, it was Paton's father who snatched her arm back before her foot touched down. It was bad luck to touch the coffin after it'd already hit the lowest part of the hole. That would mean you had two feet already in the grave. In other words, whoever touched the coffin at that point would be dying for certain really soon. Most people said it wouldn't even be two weeks before they would go on home to glory and meet the Lord.

"If you don't feel like it, Pate, I can do it later. It's just that I gotta help Mama." She turned to walk out of the room irritated but trying hard not to show it. "I don't want my own Mama to leave this earth…"

"Shut up, Janie!" Paton snapped, and she jumped at the furious sound of her brother's voice.

"Paton, what the devil put in you this morning? All I said was…"

"I heard what you said, Janie. Don't you never talk about my Mama laid up in no dirt. Never!" he slammed his fist into the wall, and a hole the size of both of his fists appeared.

"Paton!"

He jumped up from the bed, shoved Janie out of the way, so hard that her entire body slammed against the wall, and he ran out of the room. Not looking back, his eyes focused on the front door as he escaped the wounded stares of his mother when he raced beyond her room door. When he heard no calls for him to come back, he continued down the porch and ran off just to be alone.

The sun had already met the clear, blue sky at noon, and Paton was out by the creek tossing rocks on the water and watching them fall in, causing the water to ripple. His heart was heavy as he looked over across the water and at the cemetery where Drowning Boy was buried. He could even see where the dirt hadn't settled on the ground yet.

Tears began to well up in his eyes once again, and he felt secure enough to let them fall because no one was around to watch him mourn. In the back of his mind, the voice of Ethel Washington, Drowning Boy's mother, continued to hound him ever since he heard her screaming and sobbing over her son. The way Drowning Boy's blood smeared across her face as she laid her head on his chest brought back the memories of how close Drowning Boy was with his mother. They would have died for one another.

His mind then wandered to how if it would not have been for Drowning Boy's shooting, he would have had another sister, but that white man took the life of his sister, too. He may not have shot her, but he may as well had put bullet holes in her, too. As he cringed at the side of the creek while his rage rose up to greet his heart with vengeance, he also blamed that same white man for the near death of his mother who dragged herself down the road in agony to claim his own life from a possible lynching.

Nothing would ever be the same. His father was right. It had nothing to do with a sign but everything to do with that white man hating them so much that they couldn't even walk through the fields anymore. Paton remembered what the man with the gun said to him before Drowning Boy died from his wound, about him not wanting Coloreds on the grounds at all, like a white man's feet were somehow better than his…how a Colored man's blood would destroy the crops…

Because Paton had never in his life come across a hatred so deathly before his very eyes, he didn't know how to just take it and continue to live like his father directed him to do. He wanted to fight. His mom's words plagued him like a never ending virus. She would tell him to keep away from the source of the pain and the pain would leave with prayer, but all Paton thought about doing was returning to the spot where his friend died just to wait…wait on what to do next.

As he fumbled along the water, he removed a box of matches from his pocket and began to slide one of the matches slowly against the rough side of the box. He didn't want to strike the match at all, but many times, Paton would fiddle with things when he had much on his mind. This particular time, the matches did the trick as he walked underneath the shade of the trees all alone. He heard the birds chirping, and whenever the wind blew, he felt like he was betraying both his dead sister and Drowning Boy because he could still feel the wind. His sister never had a chance to feel it, and Drowning Boy wouldn't ever be able to feel the wind again.

"Paton," someone called.

Paton turned around at the sound of Jesse's voice. He was running up behind him quickly but began to slow up as got closer to the water's edge. As soon as Paton laid his blurry eyes on him, he wiped his eyes, took a deep breath and turned around.

"You 'bout to fish out here today? It's too hot, Jesse," he warned as he tried to behave perfectly normal, as if nothing ever happened. He hadn't spoken to Jesse ever since the killing because he was ashamed of his emotional behavior. He'd heard rumors that people were talking about how he'd turned crazy over in the fields after the shooting, and all of the talk pushed him further away from friends and family.

"I got a rod, but I ain't had nothing else to do. Stopped by your house on the way up here, but Janie said you left. Figured you came down here to the creek. If you ain't come to fish, hot or not," he asked, looking down at Paton's hands where he spotted the box of matches, "then look to me like you doing the same thing I'm doing." He sat down on the ground and stared back up at Paton. "He dead now, Pate, man." Then he stared across the water at the grave. "He gone and ain't coming back."

"And what you know?" Paton snapped while kicking at the mud beneath his feet. "You ran off and left us wit' only a story to tell everybody, and you couldn't even get that one right!"

"I been right there! I been right there and seen everything you seen. Drowning Boy was the onliest one that caught that bullet!" he shouted back at Paton, unafraid of his rant. He stood up and marched toward Paton to look him square in the face. "It don't matter if I stood ten whole feet away like you did or if'n I was thirty feet away. The facts is we both stood right where we were and ain't do much of nothin' whiles he went to His heaven. Ain't nothin' we coulda' done to stop none of it!" He turned to sit back down on the ground as his mood turned from angry to solemn. "My mom told me that we was blessed and ain't nothing woulda' changed 'cept it woulda' been three dead boys instead of one."

Paton knelt down beside his younger friend. Their eyes met, but Paton's stare won the battle as Jesse stared down at the muddy ground, starting to fiddle with the fishing rod. Then, Paton spoke up. "Ain't you rather be dead than not stand up for what you feel? Ain't you rather try to kill that man 'fore you let him just walk away like he did…him and his friend?"

"I ain't rather kill no…"

"Well, I rather!" Paton reached over and grabbed Jesse at his shoulder, but when Jesse continued to mess with his fishing rod, Paton snatched it from his hand, stood up and threw it into the creek.

"That's my daddy rod, Pate!"

"Ain't you wanna kill him?" he asked referring to the man who took Drowning Boy's life. "How our daddies and mamas walk around on this earth turning the other cheek every time one of them get outta line? That don't make no sense to me, Jess, and it ain't got no sense for your mind neither. Ain't a soul with a soul on this earth ain't feelin' what I'm feelin', but they goin' on like tomorrow will fix things when it won't! It won't, Jess!"

"What you 'specting us to do?" Jesse argued back, rolling up his pants legs to his thighs so that he can wade through the water to find his father's fishing rod. His eyes didn't even look Paton's way as he stood up from the ground once again. "We can't do nothin'. Ain't no law in this here America that care a thing 'bout us."

Paton grabbed him by his arm before he stepped into the water. "That's 'xactly what I'm talkin' 'bout. If the law ain't, we will."

"And get shot like we nearly did with them signs, Pate?" he pulled his arm back. "That's what changing the law got us. No matter how dumb the law is, to them…them with the guns and the ropes…these dumb laws look smart."

Paton stared through Jesse like he was the one who'd shot Drowning Boy, and Jesse felt it. Instead of carrying on with the conversation, Jesse put one foot inside the water, but Paton stopped him.

"I got it. You can't swim, so I don't know what you thinkin'." Paton took off his shirt being the better swimmer of anyone in his family or friends, dropped the matches on the ground, and dove in the water like a champion diver. When he was only eleven years of age, it was Paton who saved Drowning Boy from the water when he accidently slipped in one of the bigger bodies of water on the way to the coast. Other people jumped in the water to go save him, but it was Paton with his natural ability that got to him first. From there, he helped Drowning Boy to the dirt, and for about two weeks, everyone who heard of the incident called him Fish. That was Drowning Boy's third time nearly dying in the water. It seemed like death was always trying to snag Drowning Boy, and it finally got him.

Paton watched as the fishing rod floated up against the fallen moss from the hanging trees as he swam slowly over toward it. His eyes were searching for danger in the water, mainly alligators or snakes. Despite his feelings about what Jesse just said, he didn't think he could live with another friend dying by his side and he not be able to do anything. That was the sole reason he dove into the water for Jesse.

He retrieved the fishing rod after untangling the moss that had wrapped itself around it, and then slowly made his way back to the grass. While in the water, he thought about something that he'd never thought about before, and that thought was about drowning. His legs began to feel heavy and his arms like stone while his unforgiving heart created a sadness so overwhelming that he momentarily wanted to give up on his own life…until he heard Jesse call his name.

"Hey, Paton, you alright? Here, here, take this stick." He threw a large branch in the water while he held on to the other end. "Pate!"

Finally, Paton answered. "I'm alright. Cramp in my stomach. Big breakfast back at the house," he lied. "Thanks for the branch, Jesse," he stated somberly, his eyes searching the water for a way out of his life.

Jesse took the fishing rod from Paton's hand, and then backed away from the edge, giving him room to pull himself out of the water. He then handed Paton his shirt, and the box of matches fell to the ground. "What you got these matches for?"

"Ain't for nothing. Just playin' around wit' 'em. Nothin' to do."

"My pops'll kill me if something happened to this here rod. He only got one more, and that would mean he'd have to go fishin' by hisself."

Although Paton was wet from head to toe, he grabbed his shirt from the ground and shoved it back over his head as the scorching sun already started to dry him off. He then reached down to get the matches that fell off his shirt and were laying in the grass.

"This what you came out here to do?" Paton asked while it was fairly obvious that he had nothing left to say to Jesse. "You came out here to pretend…pretend that this here stuff we got to live through is just fine, huh?" Jesse didn't respond. Instead he cast the line into the water, and Paton continued. "You do that. I can't. I won't. If somebody hurt me, then they deserve to hurt back."

Paton left Jesse right where he was, holding the fishing rod, and as he walked off, he could feel Jesse's eyes on him. He didn't turn back around though. Part of him didn't even blame Jesse because who didn't want to forget about hard times and just fish and be young? If all that happiness had to come with pretending, Paton didn't want any part of it. It had to be one or the other. There was no in between. There would never be anymore pretending, not in his world.

As Paton neared the end of the pathway, he turned to only see Jesse still standing there with his head forward. The fishing line looked like it was still in the water, but inside of Paton, he felt like Jesse wasn't thinking about the rod nor watching the line. Just like he said, it was too hot to fish. Paton knew Jesse was staring at that grave, and deep down inside, he knew that Jesse felt much like he did...not alive but dead.

Finally, Paton arrived at the edge of the field where Drowning Boy was shot and stood there, his eyes going up and down the dirt boundary that separated the woods from the field that he was warned not to cross again. Each time he scanned the field, he imagined Drowning Boy laughing, racing and more through the fields that were marred in his blood. As he stood there, he even craved the sight of the man who took Drowning Boy's life. He didn't know what he would do or even say to him, but he wanted to see him again face to face.

He knew where the house was of the last owner of the land. The man who used to own the field was an old man whose family knew of the Colored people in town, just about all by name. He was always nice to everyone, Colored or the whites, which was why Paton never got into any trouble, along with anyone else, when he played his games in the field since he was a young child. Mister Hanson never hated anyone. Paton learned from his father the night Drowning Boy got killed that he and Mr. Hanson spoke one week prior, and said that he might have to sell the place and move back with his children. Turned out that the day he put it up for sale, the land was bought, and the very next day, Mr. Hanson went to be with his children before he supposedly was supposed to die. He left a note for everyone at the corner store, but he never said who bought the land. They all got the answer with Drowning Boy a little too late.

Paton changed the direction of his feet and started walking toward where he knew the old owner lived. He figured, if he sold the land, then he sold the house, too. It was there that he would find the new owner, and maybe even the man who killed Drowning Boy.

It only took him about twenty to thirty minutes to reach the house that he'd never even gotten that close to ever in his life. The house was one of the biggest he'd ever seen on that side of the field, and he had to walk the long way around just to get there because of the warning that he was given the last time. As he kneeled behind a pine tree, he watched as the birds flew back and forth from a bird's house that sat on the porch. The steps were painted white along with the railings, and although the wood's true color shown through, anyone could tell from miles away that pride was taken in the appearance of the house.

There was nothing going on at the home. Paton sat and watched for twenty minutes, and as the thin clouds kept moving in the sunny sky, he stood up from his position and walked forward. Having seen nothing threatening, he wanted to find out if anyone was at home, and as he walked forward, his eyes did the opposite. They continuously moved side to side, awaiting the worst to happen as his heart thumped faster and faster. The worst never came, and by the time his eyes stopped moving, he was on the front porch standing directly at the front door. Paton's breathing grew strong and his fists heavy as he went to knock, but instead, he turned the knob. It remained silent the entire time it turned until, finally, it opened, and he dropped the knob. The door slowly fell open without a sound until it stopped moving. Paton's lungs stopped taking in air, and the muscles in his arm tensed up from believing that he was about to see the man who he knew as a murderer standing before him. The place was empty however. Paton then made his way inside, closing the door behind him.

There was no odor in the house, and everything was scattered about, just like if someone was just moving in or just moving out. It was good that the outside of the house was impressive because the inside was quite the opposite. As Paton took one step after another, some slowly and some quicker than others, he made his way to the hall and then to the back rooms. There were only four. He looked back at the front door and then back ahead of himself as he kept moving, remembering another way out that he saw as he passed by the kitchen which was to his right.

Each room he passed looked ghostly. Both of the front rooms were empty, except for a large sheet that spread the floor of one of them and a chair that sat in the middle of the floor of the other. As he crept to the back rooms, he stopped in the middle of the hallway at a sound that rocked his balance. Grabbing the wall, he placed his back against it and slid down the rest of the hall as quietly as he could. There was a man snoring inside the room, and as Paton leaned over and peered in the room through the crack at the hinges of the door, there he was. It was the same man. It was the same one who shot Drowning Boy. The hair on his face was the same which made Paton certain of his identification. It was the man named Tommy. He looked around in the room the best that he could, but then he heard another sound, a grown man grunting, coming from a room he didn't check – the bathroom.

Immediately, Paton sneaked out of the house as fast as he could through the side door that he glanced at earlier. When he shut the door, he dashed out to an area behind the house and sat, listening to hear what he could hear. He nervously began to rub his hands together, thinking hard about what he needed to do, but then he stopped wondering as he reached inside his pocket.

There was some dried up leaves in the back with some wood that looked like it'd been sitting there ever since the winter months. Everything was sitting right up against the house alongside Paton, and as he started to look around beyond the trees that were directly in front of him, he carved a pathway with his eyes that he would run to get back to the creek. As Paton's heart raced, he again thought of all the pain and agony Drowning Boy went through while they let him die a horrible and unmerciful death, and he struck the match, not caring at all about who else was in the home with the killer he knew as Tommy. While holding it down into the leaves, he set it aflame. Paton stood there for minutes and watched the flames as they caught hold to the small wooden porch. That was when he left, running into the woods, but when he got there, he turned back around while hiding behind a tree. He needed to make sure the flames got the people inside. That was what he wanted most of all...for them to just die.

When the smoke started to rise and no one came from the house, he looked down at the match that he used to make the fire. It was still in between his fingertips. He put it in his pocket and ran off back down to the creek. His mind, which had been going crazy ever since the shooting, felt relieved, and much of his rage subsided despite knowing that he'd done the thing that his mother and even God would hate the most – revenge.

As he drew closer to the creek, he stopped to look over the trees at smoke that started to fill the air. There wasn't much of it, and if he hadn't been the one to set the fire, he would never have noticed the trails of gray that floated upward over the tallest of the trees from so far away. When he got to where he saw the edge of the creek where most would normally fish, there was Jesse still there, sitting down on the dirt with his father's rod leaning over toward the water.

Paton shoved the matches deeper into his pocket and the one he used to set the house on fire, he gripped in the palm of his hand. As he approached Jesse from behind, he thought that he'd gone unnoticed, but he was wrong.

"We got to get through this one, Pate. Ain't no way we can live like this here." Jesse didn't even turn around to face Paton, and at the sound of Jesse's voice, Paton stopped walking for a moment. Then, he took a deep breath and walked up beside Jesse.

"I know. We do have to get over it somehow," he said, feeling a rush of emotional freedom for the first time since the time he watched Drowning Boy suffocate on his own blood while two white men stood there like it was something funny to do. Each time his mind went back there, the angrier he became, and he looked up at the sky waiting for the light gray smoke to turn jet black which would mean the whole house went up, and hopefully them with it. He glanced down at Jesse who was still looking straight ahead, and continued to talk, "You know I told him a long time back when we was just kids that we was gonna look after each other. Well, he kinda told me that, and I agreed to the deal. Back there in them fields, I ain't do a good job looking after him, Jesse, but he did a good job looking out for me 'cause I'm the one here. He over there," he stated, referring to Drowning Boy's grave.

"I miss him, Pate," Jesse stated, holding back the tears that had already started streaming on the inside of his body. "I can remember when they shot, and I turned 'round behind them trees. He was standing there for only a second or two at the mostest when he fell right down. He ain't want us to die. He was tellin' us to run, and it wasn't 'til I was sleep in my bed that I'd seen what he'd done. He was fightin' 'em back so we could live, and it ain't right what they done, Pate. It just ain't! He ain't break no law that bad...we ain't do nothin' that bad to 'serve what we got for it. That there land ain't even his! It ain't even his, Pate."

Finally, Jesse's tears came gushing down his cheeks, and all Paton could do was sit there with him until they all faded away because he couldn't cry anymore.

"I remember, Jesse. That land there belonged to his cousin, but as far as I know, all of 'em hate us, so they all the same and would do the same just because they want to."

Just as Paton was responding, Jesse jumped up from the ground and pointed over toward the direction from where Paton ran from. "Look there. What's that coming up in the sky there? That's a fire, Pate." He dropped the fishing rod, placed a rock on top of the handle, and then ran quickly forward, about six steps way from Paton. Instead of moving, Paton sat there for a couple seconds, pretending like he didn't see anything, but he saw. The smoke was just like he wanted it to be, and while Jesse marveled at the smoke, Paton stared over at Drowning Boy's grave.

"I did it, DB," Paton whispered to himself as he rose from the ground. Jesse was so engulfed in where the smoke was coming from that he didn't hear him confess. "I got him back. Same way you had my back over there, I got him back. Burnin'…just like your mom want him to…on top of the earth and in the earth. They gone burn."

"Paton, hey man, come and see this now. We got to go over there, see if we can help put it out. Ain't nobody 'round here close to put out no fires, so come on. We can't wait no longer 'cause you see how black that smoke is?" When Jesse turned around, beckoning him to come, he saw Paton standing there without any efforts on running. "Paton…" he uttered, confused as to why he wasn't coming. Any other time, Paton would have been the first one to bolt out and help somebody with just about anything. Aside from his joking attitude most of the time, he was just as helpful, outside of his temper.

"Let's go then," Paton started after stalling.

"You alright?" Jesse turned all the way around, staring at Paton questionably.

"You leavin' your daddy's rod here?" Paton asked only to change the subject. It worked.

"Yeah, yeah, it's alright. Ain't nobody coming to fish this time a day but me," Jesse hesitantly responded to his question because he knew that Paton was well aware of the times most people would come to the creek anyway, and when they did come, everyone knew his father's rod. Even though Jesse felt uneasy about Paton's behavior, he shrugged it off as being a result of Drowning Boy. "Let's go."

They both ran off, Jesse in his normal quickness and Paton at an abnormal speed. Paton ran behind Jesse and watched as Jesse constantly turned around to see if he was still behind him. The closer Jesse got to the burning house, however, the slower Paton got, until he came to a standstill within about one hundred feet from the flames. When Jesse turned back around, he stopped in his race to rescue and stared at his friend who was a good distance behind him standing in the woods. He looked around himself because Paton's stare made him feel paranoid. Quickly, he hopped back behind the trees and walked slowly toward him, feeling the immense heat from the fire that was overtaking the house.

Paton just stood there. His head was facing Jesse, but his eyes penetrated the house that was covered in black smoke. His fists clenched underneath the trees, and his chest no longer looked like one of an innocent boy. It looked like the chest of a fighter, someone who was prepared for battle and waiting for the final fight. Paton's face was drenched with sweat, but he didn't wipe one drop from it. Other than the obvious anxiety that being in the area brought him, he was frozen like a statue.

Jesse crept up closer, realizing that something was very wrong. "Paton," he said as he carefully reached out to his shoulder. Although he barely touched it, Paton jerked away and glared at him as if he'd committed the worst offense. Jesse jumped away, startled as he glanced from Paton to the torched house then back at Paton until he remembered something that he'd seen at the creek. "Paton…hey, man?" he stammered, unsure of himself or what to say next. "Where them matches at, Pate?"

Paton failed to answer him, and then he turned his head back to watch the home burn. His eyes shifted to the front of the home and then back to the back, but he saw no one escape and heard no one yelling for help. Then, he looked back into a terrified Jesse's eyes; he looked like he'd seen the dead walking.

"Ain't no sense in going over there to put nothing out. You hear somebody?" he asked, waiting on Jesse to answer, but he never did. Paton noticed Jesse's breathing, and then reached out to pull him closer, but Jesse stumbled backward.

"You done set this place a'fire, didn't you, Pate?" he asked in a tone so low that it could barely be heard. Although it was hot where he stood, Jesse felt like the whole earth suddenly got cold as he waited for Paton's answer to the question.

"He killed Drowning Boy…that same man was in there," Paton finally stated. "Shot him in the back, and the bullet came straight out his stomach. Then he hit him and just let him die. Ain't care none, and he did that for a colored boy walkin' on his family field. I had to pull blood from his mouth while he choked to death on it. I ain't tell you that, did I?" He then looked back at the smoldering wooden house being taken by flames. "Ain't it fittin' for them to burn? The fire can't be too wrong, can it, Jesse? Or is it that fire is worse than that bullet? Huh? Which one did worse? This here fire or the bullet?"

"You done gone crazy, Pate." Jesse backed up further from him. "You set that man on fire? This his family house you set on fire with them matches? You can't go 'round hatin' like them folk! It's you that'll die…"

"I ain't hatin' like them, and I ain't dyin' like them either!" he stated, referring to the men burning in the house. "Is that what you think? Come here and looks at what I see," he ordered, leaping forward and grabbing Jesse at the shirt and tugging him down to the ground with him. They both kneeled and gazed at the house. "I ain't hatin' them because of they color like they do me, you and the rest of us. They color ain't got nothin' to do with it." Then, he fiercely pulled out the matches from his pocket as Jesse stared in horror, unable to make himself run away because he wouldn't know what to do or say to anyone if he did. Paton continued, "I can't hate them like they hate us. I hate them 'cause of what they…that family…did to my friend! He was my friend!" he moaned as tears welled up in his eyes and began to fall like rain in a heavy storm. Then, he wiped his eyes and lifted the matches in front of his eyes and continued, "And now, I'm gonna watch them burn to death for it, just like they did my friend."

Jesse began to try and knock Paton's hand away from his shirt frantically, but Paton was holding on so tight that he ripped it just to get away from him. Then, he stood up in great fear as Paton stared him in his eyes and warned him…

"Don't tell a soul, Jesse. This ain't nobody's business. Take it to the grave…"

"What you do this to me for? You can't just land a curse on me like this and tell me to keep it!"

Paton stood up right in front of him, unmoved by what he said because as far as Paton was concerned, the only curse there was burning up in the house. He responded, "I walked through there, Jesse, right before I did it. I saw the man laying in the bed in the back room. He was breathing. How he get to kill Drowning Boy and ain't nothing done to him? I had to set it on fire," he said turning back to face the flames. "If you gonna tell somebody on me, then tell. I did what I had to do…for Drowning Boy. You do what you gotta do for yourself, but live wit' it though. Live wit' it."

Paton didn't even have to turn around before he heard Jesse take back off through the woods. The sight of the house burning felt like closure to something he didn't finish as his friend died in his arms. Finally, he lifted his shirt to his face and wiped from top to bottom, sat back down on the ground, and waited until he saw people come running from the road to save anything that was left. It took hours to put the fire out because of where the house was located, but when they were just about done, Paton got up and left, undetected by anyone who was around. He never saw the man he aimed to kill come out alive nor the other man who just happened to be in the bathroom at the time.

By the time Paton got back to the creek, Jesse was long gone and so was that fishing rod. He didn't see anybody on a massive search for him, so he assumed that Jesse kept his mouth closed although he'd already made himself ready to be punished for his crime. As he walked, he crossed over a raggedy low bridge that connected hard grounds from a patch of mud that never seemed to dry up and walked briskly to Drowning Boy mother's house. The sun was on its way down, so Paton knew that he had to hurry.

He'd been gone all the day long, and his father was going to have plenty questions.

The front porch of Mrs. Ethel Washington's house was repainted since Drowning Boy died. The color of it was a darker brown to go on top of the lighter brown that it once was. Painting was a hobby of Mrs. Washington's. She would say she did it to keep her mind off of her deceased husband's passing because she was able to do what he liked to do. Changing the color of the house every year was his hobby, so she would do the same thing just to make believe he was still there. She would even go to the same place where they dumped the paint buckets, carry them back to the house, and mix the paint with water until she got the color she wanted.

As he walked up the front porch, the house seemed to be empty. When he knocked on the door, he waited for one whole minute, but no one came to answer. Feeling uneasy again, he went around to the side of the house to where Drowning Boy's room used to be. His window was always left open, and Mrs. Ethel knew that was how he would sometimes come into the house, through Drowning Boy's window. He'd been doing that for years, and it was nothing to Mrs. Washington. Sometimes she would even walk by Drowning Boy's room door without looking inside and ask how Paton's parents were doing because she knew he would be in there.

Even though Drowning Boy was gone, his window was still left open as usual. Therefore, Paton climbed on inside, looking for a pencil to write with and a scrap piece of paper. Underneath Drowning Boy's bed was where he kept papers he would practice drawing on, so he knelt down to get the paper and pencil that sat on top of it. Then, he turned around and sat on the floor of the untouched room and began writing a note on a blank sheet of paper.

IT'S DONE. I SENT HIM TO HELL FOR WHAT HE DID, AND NOW YOU AND DROWNING BOY CAN REST IN PEACE. HE BURNIN.

Paton dug inside his pocket quickly after writing the note and put the match inside the paper, folded it up and walked out of Drowning Boy's room into the hallway. He faced Mrs. Washington's room door which was completely shut. Therefore, he leaned over and shoved the note underneath her door and rushed to leave out the same way he came inside, not knowing that Drowning Boy's mother was inside.

At the sound of the note underneath the door, Mrs. Washington rose from her weeping sleep. After looking around in the room and calling for her son, she saw the piece of torn off paper and stopped, hesitant to move forward.

"William? William, baby?" Suddenly, she dropped to her bare knees, scrambling for the piece of paper that, in the back of her mind, came from her dead son somehow. She picked it up and fell back onto her backside not able to focus on the words too well after crying too much, but when the words came into focus, there was a change in her expression. Her sorrow fled and anger blazed inside her veins before satisfaction found a dwelling place on her face. She rose up from her seat on the floor, walked steadily back to the bed she'd laid on for hours at a time during the day, and sat down on the thin, white sheets. The signature on the bottom of the note read the letter P and the burnt match told her all she needed to know. In an unremorseful state, Mrs. Washington ripped the paper up in her lap, and one piece after another with the match going first, she ate the evidence until there was nothing left.

Paton was never caught for his deeds that smoldering, summer day because Jesse never told a soul. Eventually,

Jesse started to feel the same way Paton felt, and if he didn't really feel that way, he did a good job pretending. The both of them appeared to have pushed it out of their minds, but appearances weren't always a truth teller. As far as Paton, he may have set those men in that house on fire, causing those acres of fields to free back up into someone else's hands, but his mind wasn't set free as much as he thought it was.

His father John Lee, died years afterward from lumps that were growing inside his body that he never told anybody about, not even his wife Sarah. He just kept getting weaker and weaker until his body gave out one day which left Paton in charge of everything, including the earnings as he grew into his mid-twenties in age. Being at that point a young, strong man, he could work for hours beyond the full day and have energy to spare. He would bring the money home to his sister Janie and his mom until his mom passed away only a couple years after his father. Sarah caught some virus that she never recovered from, but on her death bed she leaned in to whisper something into Paton's ear which made him shudder with fear. She told him that she knew he burned those men alive, and she'd already begged the Lord for his forgiveness. Then she pleaded with him again to keep his temper, or it was gonna take his life from him, turn him into a monster.

"Don't let this life here make you hate, folk. Heartache comes, but you gotta guard your heart so it won't take your love from you, son. God ain't a liar. You have to believe…" That was when her head dropped backwards onto Paton's arm, and he cried for countless days until he met the love of his life later on down the line. She would ease his pain, but only for some time.

THE MAN

"Hey, who's that there, Tunk?"

"Man, pay attention to this here paint 'fore you knock it over. I ain't got you this job to have you mess it up for me behind lookin' at somebody you ain't gone get."

Paton climbed down off the ladder and went over and nudged the man that was able to get him steady work. He didn't need much to care for himself and his sister Janie because she worked as a helper in someone's kitchen. Together, they made a good team since the death of their parents. Paton was used to living off of a little at a time, so whatever extra he got, he saved because his father always told him that hard times were bound to come. It was important to be ready for them. Therefore, that was what Paton and Janie did, and it was like second nature.

"No, man, I'ma get her. You know her?" he asked Tunk, continuing to jab him in the arm.

"Know her? I went to grade school with her 'fore I dropped out. She name Rain. We used to pick on her and say how come your mama ain't named you snow?"

Paton walked around Tunk while keeping his eyes on the young lady across the street who was picking flowers from a garden with two other ladies. "It don't matter what you call her," he stated, moving his straw hat up from his forehead so he would watch Rain in her yellow dress. "That there is gonna be my lady right there. Watch this."

"Yeah, man, Mr. Heights coming back and we need to have this part done by sunset," Tunk complained, but his complaints fell on deaf ears as Paton was already crossing the street, using a towel to wipe the sweat from his face. Tunk just shook his head as he watched Paton. "She gone turn him flat down," he mumbled, taking a seat on one of the bricks so he could prepare himself for a good laugh.

Paton slid him a glance as he turned his head to the side to inconspicuously look back, but at the same time, keep his eyes on what he considered his prize. He wasn't going to allow his boss or Tunk stop him from what could be a once in a lifetime opportunity. As far as the people he went to school with, he didn't like any of the girls much, mainly because he grew up with them, and it felt awkward. He would have a crush every now and then, but he never stuck with the girl after courting them. Paton's whole idea of a woman was someone whom he could learn about from square one. He loved the chase and the mystery, and no females he knew gave him that... except for Rain.

Rain was already kneeling down to pick another flower when one of her friends tapped her on the waist, alerting her to a man standing right behind her. Slightly startled, she turned around, first to her friend and then to the man standing a bit off to her side.

"Excuse me, y'all," Paton started, removing his hat from his head, "Mind if I talk to this young lady right here by myself for a minute?"

The ladies smiled a bit, and so did Rain, but not much. She was a woman who knew her worth. Therefore, she couldn't be taken by a slick tongue easily. That was the least of her problems, however, because when she looked at Paton, she was instantly attracted to his muscular frame, bold attitude and the faultless smile that only added to his walnut toned skin that made him flawless under the sun. Even though she tried not to do so, Rain's stowick expression was dismantled as she became flattered that he stopped by.

Paton assumed his position up against a fence to look Rain over as she continued to behave as if she wasn't attracted to the man that stood before her. Before she even picked another flower, Paton leaned over and collected five more for her, twisted the stems together and knotted the bottom, something he's watched his sister Janie do many times with his mother.

"How about that?" he asked Rain, believing that he'd impressed her with his floral design. "May I?" he asked, referring to her wrist. Rain simply lifted her arm, and he tied it on her wrist lightly. "You make those flowers beautiful. What's your name?"

"Name's Rain."

"As in rain that comes from the sky?"

"Yeah, that kinda rain," she giggled.

"Where you get a name like that from, Ms. Rain?" he asked, looking at her ring finger to be sure she wasn't married or about to be doing so.

"Of course, my mom gave it to me when I was born," she says sarcastically, "Just like your mom gave you your name when you came out as well."

"Ain't you gonna ask me what it is?"

She looked back at him, and then she glanced over at her friends who'd taken a seat beneath a nearby tree. They were pointing and whispering, but that was when Paton broke her stare by moving into her line of vision.

"Here, lemme get that for you." He reached for her basket of flowers, and she allowed him to take it.

"It sure does look mighty funny you taking a basket of flowers on your arm, don't you think?"

"Not for you it don't. Even if it did, I don't mind looking crazy for you, Ms. Rain. Listen here, I'm about to get off now," he lied. "You mind leaving your friends and letting me take care of you for the day?"

"You got that much time on your hands?"

"I makes time." He looked back over at Tunk who was busy doing nothing except looking his way and yelled across the street, "I'm sick. Ms. Rain here said she gonna make me some tea," he said, glancing back at her, "To make me feel better." Then he continued to shout, "Tell boss man I'll be back tomorrow."

"What you say now? Come on, man! This too much work over here!" Tunk shouted. "This here is more money, Pate!"

He glanced at Rain who was shocked he was about to leave his job to be with her for the day. Her eyes were wide open as her hand covered her mouth in laughter which made Paton even happier to leave all his work back there with Tunk. "You got some pretty eyes, Rain."

She removed her hand from her mouth, placed her hand back on her basket, taking it from his possession, and said, "Thank you...but you better get back to work."

"You rather me get back to work so you can get back to pickin' daises? You sho' you don't want me to talk to you for a while?" he asked with a smile on his face that made Rain melt down so much that she couldn't answer. He winked at her and then back at Tunk. "I'll be back tomorrow!"

Rain looked over at her friends who'd stood up at the tree with their hands out at their sides waiting on her to finish with her conversation, but she simply shrugged her shoulders while they started jumping up and down. Paton happened to see the commotion as he took the basket of flowers back from her hand to start picking handfuls of flowers as they started walking down the road. Tunk continued to call him, but both Paton and Rain decided not to hear him.

"So your name's Pate?"

"Is that what you heard that man back there call me? Pate?"

"Sure...ain't that what he said?"

"Guess it is, but that ain't my name. The full thing is Paton. Folks sometimes call me Pate for short, folks who known me long. You can call me what you want to, Rain. You from 'round here because I ain't never seen you."

"Yeah, I'm from here, just not on this side. On the other side of town. Went to school with Tunk back there, you know."

"Yeah?"

"You act like he didn't tell you before you came to see about me?"

Paton laughed while he became taken by Rain's beauty. Not only was she very pretty in his sight, but she was witty as well. It wasn't easy to make Paton feel shy or uneasy, but in this case, it was a feeling to which he wasn't accustomed, thus, making him a bit out of control of the conversation. He wasn't used to that.

"Yeah, tell you the truth, he did tell me about you."

"Did he volunteer, or was it you that asked?"

"I asked. Soon as I saw you…" he answered with his head down, feeling far different than he'd ever felt about a woman a day in his life. He wasn't extremely comfortable with his current emotions, but instead of running from them, he decided to continue to sort them out. "You hungry? I can run on over to the shop across the street, and get us something."

"I am a little hungry after being out all morning…" she answered when he cut her off.

"You don't have to say nothin' else, Rain. Come on over here," he requested. There was nice, low cut grass in a make shift park for the kids to play in over the summer time, but since school wasn't quite out yet, Paton figured that he could steal it just for himself and his new love interest.

"To the park?"

"Yeah, is it something wrong with sittin' over here with me at the park under this tree here?"

She laughed, "No, ain't nothing wrong with it."

"Come on then." He touched her hand softly and she accepted his touch by losing herself in his deep, brown eyes and touching his hand back. They both walked silently over into the empty park, and the only thing on Paton's mind was that he had possibly fallen in love at first sight.

With each step, Paton watched how she moved. Whether Rain noticed he was watching or not, Paton was sold on the fact that she was the most lovely lady to ever cross his path or hold his hand. Her dress was yellow, and it flowed down to her ankles and feet where he saw that they looked just as soft as her hands felt.

As he reached the portion of the grass underneath a tree, he stopped Rain in her gait. "Will you wait a second right here? Let me do something for you."

"Do something like what?" she asked, impressed by how she was being treated by him.

"I can't have you sittin' on the grass in your nice dress," he answered, kneeling down and spreading all the flowers that she'd picked on the ground. There were so many that as he spread them out, it covered the grassy area like a sheet. "Go ahead and have a seat, Rain." He stood up and took her hand again. "I just needed to make you a seat. No woman of mine will ever have to sit on the bare ground, not long as I'm able to do something about it."

She smiled again, truly at a loss for words, but instead of remaining captivated by the man she was trying hard to figure out, she challenged his generosity. "I needed those flowers. They're for my cousin's wedding, and I don't want to sit on them…"

Paton grabbed her other hand and interrupted quietly as he leaned over near her ear where he smelled the freshness of her clean hair that draped her shoulders in a multitude of curls. "I promise I'll pick you another full basket 'fore the sun goes down, just the way you want me to pick 'em. Whatever color you want, I'll find 'em. Whatever size you want…I'll even buy 'em," he whispered. "Just sit down for me, Ms. Rain, while I go get us somethin' to eat. You do that for me?"

Rain removed herself from his grasp slowly and took a seat atop the sheet of flowers. As soon as Paton saw that she was comfortable and safe, he ran off to the store to buy something to eat as fast as he could. Just before he stepped onto the street, he heard Tunk again calling his name from far off, and he waved his hand and yelled back, "I'm off!" He crossed the street and entered the small store where there were about five men out front. Noticing that he was all sweaty and filthy from working all morning, he pulled out thirty cents.

"Hey there now…any one of you lemme have the shirt off your back. I got a young pretty one back there waitin' on me."

"Shoot yeah, you can have this'un here for thirty whole cents! It's clean as a whistle. Wife washed it just yesterday, and I ain't been nowheres but here."

"Lemme get that. Thank you kindly."

He took the shirt from the man and gave him the money, then Paton walked inside the store with Rain still on his mind. With his old work shirt, he wiped his face completely clean while drying up the sweat on his arms and chest while he searched for a fresh whole peach pie along with some apples, muffins and water to wash it all down. He took everything to the counter and that was when Tunk ran through the door.

"You ain't comin' back down yonder to finish up with me? I got to do it all by my own self now?"

"Tunk, you see her, man? She over there in the park," he answered Tunk off topic and so full of excitement that his breathing was erratic. "Man, she nice and the best lookin' girl I seen in a long time round here, Tunk. Job or no job, I gots plenty money saved, 'tween me and you, and I ain't coming back…not today. I'm sick, T."

"My head gonna be on the choppin' block for this…"

"How, Tunk? He ain't gonna be back 'til time to leave anyway. Just tell him I got sick. Move now. I got to go. Tell you 'bout it in the morning, and I'll make it up to ya, do double the work includin' yours."

"Includin' mine?"

"Yours," he stressed getting the food together in a bag with something to eat with and napkins.

"Hopes you ain't wastin' all that money."

"It's mo' where that came from. I lives off nothing, but I got enough to go 'round if need be. Tomorrow!" he called, walkin' out the door, but then he turned back around. "Hey, Tunk…I stink?" he asked, throwing his arm up near Tunk's nose.

"Man, move. Go on! It don't even much matter 'cause she done smelt you anyhow."

Paton laughed and ran out of the shop, hoping that Rain would still be there when he stepped out. Sure enough, she was, and he found out that his eyes hadn't betrayed him; she was just as beautiful from where he was standing. Before crossing the road, he looked both ways and headed her way, smelling himself the whole time. The problem was that he couldn't smell anything because of the peach pie's aroma covering up whatever funk his nose had already grown used to smelling.

He approached Rain with a smile, and she smiled right back. "I didn't know what you like so I got a peach pie that reminded me of how sweet you smell, and I got a couple of fresh apples and muffins with some water. Hope you eat any one of these things right here."

"I do, and I love muffins and peach pie," she responded. "Where we gonna sit it though because it can't go on the ground? The ants will start coming…"

"Lemme feed it to you…if that's alright? It don't never have to touch the ground, and your hands never have to get dirty." Paton sat on the round right beside her and continued to prove his worth. "Ain't nothin', see? I'll just sit right here beside you, hold this whole pie in one hand and feed it to you with the other."

As he spoke, Rain didn't know what to say, so she simply watched as he placed the fork inside the pie, without even cutting a slice, and lifted a nice mouthful of peaches and crust out. At first, she hesitated to take a bite, but when he nodded his head, she went ahead and took some from the fork. He watched her as she chewed, and right as she swallowed, he ate the rest from the utensil.

"How does it taste?"

"It's good. Thank you, Paton," she answered, feeling a bit embarrassed and shy because of the way he was staring at her.

"What's your last name, Rain?"

"Kennedy…Rain Kennedy," she stammered.

Paton sensed her hesitation. "What's the matter?" When she didn't respond, he continued, feeling that she might be second guessing being out there with him. "My last name's Jones. I'm from this side of the tracks, born and raised."

"Thank you for everything, Paton, but I have to…"

"Just finish talkin' with me a little bit. I won't hurt you. You got my word," he responded anxiously. "Would you like another piece?" he asked referring to the peach pie.

"Yes, I'll take another piece, but my family waitin' and…"

"I won't make you late. Here…" He leaned in to give her another slice of pie, but instead of placing it inside her mouth, he moved the fork away slowly, placed the whole pie on the flowers for a second, and with ease, placed his lips on top of hers. Paton's heart nearly skipped a beat when she kissed him back, uninhibited and unafraid. Paton's hand moved atop hers, but then suddenly, she removed her hand from underneath his.

"I'm sorry," she spoke. "I have to go."

Paton rushed to stand up at the same time she did, never once trying to force her to stay against her will. "You got nuttin' to be sorry 'bout, Rain. I'm sorry if I did somethin' you didn't want me to do. I apologize…"

"No, no…you did…" she paused, "everything I'd hoped you would do." She watched as Paton took a deep breath and then let it all out. "I like that new shirt, too," she smiled, and Paton, for the first time in front of a woman, blushed. Quickly, it faded away as he recalled the promise he made her.

"If you stay here for just a few mo', I will go get more flowers and you can be on your way. I'll even walk you where you need to go."

"You really gonna pick all them flowers again?"

"I told you I would. Be right back," he stated as he ran off with the basket. As he ran, he turned back around running backwards and shouted, "Eat all that pie 'fore the ants come! Save me an apple!"

Rain laughed as she sat back down, but the further he got away from her, the more her smile dwindled into a state of worry. By the time he got back, half the pie was gone with both apples still here and two muffins that she'd already placed back into the bag. Paton returned with double the flowers she originally had, some short and some long, but all beautiful. Then he walked her back to where her father was supposed to pick her up along with the other two ladies that were with her earlier.

"I don't think I should be with you when my father comes to get me. I'm still his baby girl, and…"

"You wasn't s'posed to be out here with me. I know. Maybe one day I can see you again. How 'bout on Saturday?" He paused and then spoke up again. "I'll come wherever you want me to come, Rain," he pleaded. "I promise. I just feel like I need to see you again is all."

"I'll be back this way then, say six o'clock?"

"In the evening…yeah, I'll be…"

"No. In the morning."

"The mornin'?"

"Yeah, the mornin'. I take the bus here so I can help out with Mrs. Lands, and I'm jus' kiddin' 'bout six. I'll be finished at ten o'clock…in the morning," she stressed. "If you meet me here?"

"Yeah, anything. I'll be here."

"Okay," she confirmed.

Without even asking, Paton leaned in once again and kissed her, first on her left cheek, and then Rain turned in and kissed him back on his lips. Paton's hand felt around her waist, and he didn't want to let go, even when he heard a car pull up on the other side of the building. Rain pulled away, and he nearly followed, until she placed her hand up to his chest to stop him. Then, she mouthed the words *ten o'clock Saturday* to him before running around to the unseen car that Paton only heard drive off. After about ten seconds, he came around the building and walked back toward Tunk who was working hard down the road. When he arrived, Tunk looked his way and shook his head.

"Done spent all your money on a woman who ain't even want you. But you sick though, so gone away now. Done started your half of the work already," he complained while joking at the same time.

"That's where you wrong, Tunk. That's gone be mine right there, and she…"

"And she what?" he asked, tossin' the paint brush at him so fast that he had to drop the bag of food to catch it.

"And I know she want me to be hers, too. That's what. You'll see. Whoooo, whoo!" he sang as he started dipping the paint brush back inside the paint. "I got a feelin', even though I just met her, she the one for me, Tunk. Gotta be."

"Well, you betta' start workin' 'fore you can't buy her no more food to sweeten her up. Her daddy real protective over her, even at her age. Ain't many people can fool him."

"Ain't nothin' to hide, Tunk. Nothin' to hide."

"Ain't nothin', Pate? You really goin' over there to that old place to fix it up all by yo'self?" Janie asked sucking on a pickled pigs foot. "What's wrong with livin' right here with me? This here our house."

"That there other one is, too, Janie. 'Sides that, I'm gettin' too old to be livin' with you. I got my own life to live," he responded quite sure of himself while he stood tall from packing a bag of workman equipment. "And you got your own to live, too. I see that old cow lookin', two legged goat you been hugged up to that call himself a man but ain't got nothin' a man s'pose to have."

"He gots just enough for me, so don't you worry yourself about him. I'm grown, and last time I checked, my daddy been dead," she retorted, putting the pig's foot back in her mouth. "If you think I'm stupid, I ain't. You act like you done got you some tail." She poked her neck out, shoving it in Paton's face. "I'm tellin' the truth, ain't I? You did, didn't you?"

"You need to go somewhere and brush them gums is what you need to do instead of askin' me about what I got and don't got," he laughed. "I got me a woman, and I'm gonna meet her family soon, so I got to have everything right."

"A woman?" she stood up with her chest poked out. "You thinkin' 'bout marrying?" A huge grin molded upon her face, and then she erupted in laughter as she held her pig's foot in her left hand while her right hand remained attached to her hip. After pretending like she was choking off of the juices from the foot, she pulled up her skirt and placed her bare foot on the bottom of a stool.

Paton simply continued to do what he was doing, fairly accustomed to the antics of his sister. "I hear you laughing, but soon, you may have yourself a sister in law. You hear that?"

"What's her name, Pate?" she asked, settling down to try and get all the information that she could about the budding relationship.

"Name's Rain, and 'fore you even say it, yeah, it's like the rain that come down from the sky."

"With thunder and lighting and hail...that kinda rain?"

Paton stopped, walked over to her and stared her straight in the eyes. "Naw, not like that rain, but a sweet, summer day kinda rain, where it comes down soft, just enough so that we won't drought out but not too much that it won't be like the days of Noah. That kinda rain." After saying what he had to say, he backed up with his eyes still on Janie and said, "Unlike you...a hurricane on a nice, sunny day."

"Shut up, Paton! Stupid self!" She threw the pig's foot his way, and he ducked as it landed on the other side of the porch. "When I'ma meet this Rain?"

"When I feel like you need to..."

"When is that gonna be?"

He tossed the bag of equipment over his shoulder and replied with certainty, "Soon as she say yes." He then turned around on one heel, paused, and then turned back to face her overstretched eyes. "And she will be sayin' yes, sister. Mark

73

my words on my good mama and daddy grave she will. I'm gone see to that." He then turned back around to walk to his father's old shack to fix it up like it had never been fixed before.

"Alright na'. Don't make me lay hands across your face for puttin' mama and daddy in your lil' dumb affairs."

Paton paid her no attention as he continued on his way to the shack that wasn't too far down the road. Periodically, he would think about going over there alone. The problem was that it would bring back his father's memory because he would always be with him to visit the place. Most times after his father's death, Paton would walk just close enough to make sure nobody was living in it, cut the grass down around the area to make it appear lively, and even cut some of the bushes. This particular time though, Paton had enough desire to overcome his lingering hesitation to enter the old shack and make a home of it before his planned meeting with Rain's father.

As he walked onward, he thought about how strong a father he had, and how he one day wanted to emulate him as much as possible, be the man his dad always wanted him to be. Passing through the sweat-carved path his father created when he was only ten years old, he began to speak to his deceased father as if he was right there beside him.

"Pop, I'm lookin' to marry a girl I done met the other day. S'pose to be meetin' her on Saturday again, so til then, I want to work as much as possible to get this old shack fixed up. I know I hadn't been inside much since you left here, but it's a time for everything, right?" he paused, expecting an answer somewhere inside his soul. Instead of getting the answer he'd hoped for, he imagined his father answering. "I know, I know, it's a lil' soon to be talking about marriage, but I know she the one, pops. Tunk thinks I'm crazy, but I ain't. I'm gonna do just like you said," he continued, stopping directly in front of the small, wooden house. "I'm gonna prove I can take care of her to myself and then her poppa, then I'ma have to prove it to God when I take that oath." He dropped his bag on the ground and stretched his arms. "She gone be mine. Rain shole is gone be..."

"'Bout time you got here!" Tunk yelled through the open window of the shack. "If you stop talkin' to yourself, maybe we can get this here floor cleaned up by sundown."

"Tunk! Man, you showed up!" Paton responded happily, grabbing his bag from the ground and running up to the broken porch.

Tunk wrestled with a weed that hung from his mouth and then spit it on the ground before answering. "You didn't think I was gonna let you look like a plum fool outch'here, did ya? It takes more than two hands and some man in love to do this here kinda work. 'Sides that, if I can work for the man out yonder all day long for that lil bit of change he put in my pocket, I can shole work for a friend for free on our day off."

"Well, I do thank ya. Didn't think I would see you here after all that laughin' you did at me." Paton stared around at the debris that created a dump for scenery. "Hey, Tunk?"

"Yeah, it's a wreck in here. You ain't got to ask," he responded, guessing that the filthy shack was what Paton was going to ask about.

"I already know that. Man, I'm talkin' 'bout Rain," he said, tying up his shoes and pulling out a sander, hammer and nails, and some rope from the satchel. "Think she gonna stay interested...I mean her pops there...because I gotta impress her and the rest of her family? Ain't no man 'gone approve of no man with nothing for they daughter, ain't that right?"

"Tell ya' the truth, I shole wouldn't. Get this place fixed up nice, she nor her ole daddy can't say no. That's all a family need, right? God, a man, woman, chillin' running round and food to eat and water to wash!"

"You know them Kennedys good?"

"Just Rain. I hear though that her family got some snot on they nose, but they fine by me. Way I see it, a family that work hard for what they got, need it and shouldn't nobody shame 'em for it long as they got it the right way. They a hard working family is what I know. All them Kennedys, but that was way back then though. Used to hear my folks talk 'bout 'em from time to time, and that's what they say. You ready?"

"Yeah, I'm ready," Paton dragged his voice. Although he'd asked the question about Rain and her people, he never thought that it would make him feel so out of place and nearly impossible to ask for her hand in marriage some day. He entered the old shack that Tunk had obviously started on and got to work until sun down, and by Saturday morning, although he was in much physical pain for overworking, he still got up out of bed, cleaned himself up and met who he saw as his bride to be.

Right back where Paton left Rain, there he saw her again from down the road. Before he stepped out to go meet her down the street, he hesitated, figuring that he better wait on her to reach him as he didn't know who could have been watching. As he waited, he smelled himself over and rubbed is face that he shaved really good with the razor early that morning. His sister Janie got up with him and even checked him over to make sure his appearance was to a female's liking. She would always say that a man knew what a man liked but never what a woman liked because they tended to think it was the same as what a man wanted which it wasn't. Therefore, because she loved her brother so, she wanted him to sweep Rain off of her feet, regardless of if she liked her or not – having never met her yet. Her sole objective was to keep her brother happy because for years, it had secretly bothered her about everything he had to endure, so much so that she'd started drinking behind closed doors, just enough to ease the pain of his pain and the pain of losing her parents. The sips of wine would keep a smile on her face at all times, thus Paton's.

"You better be right, Janie. I shoulda' brought her something," he said to himself after remembering how his sister told him not to take Rain anything for fear of her fallin' in love with the gifts and not the man behind the gifts. "Ain't no tellin' what she expect since this date was a planned thing."

Paton put on his best clothes for the outing. He wore a shirt and pants made for only the church, and his shoes were brown to the shine he gave them the night before. The shoes used to belong to his father, and he only wore them on special occasions. This just happened to be one of those occasions.

Standing at the corner of the brick wall, he continued to watch anxiously as Rain got closer, until he heard someone calling his name. He turned around quickly only to see his sister Janie, leaned over on top of a huge tree stump.

"Janie, what you want?" He leaned over, picked up a small rock from the ground, and threw it her way as a sign for her to leave. She didn't.

"I got to see who she is, Paton, is all. Can't I do that? Ain't had no business telling me. Is that her?"

Paton turned back to face Rain as she smiled back at him and waved. He waved back as calmly as he could, but he couldn't concentrate on being the man he wanted to portray because Janie was still talking.

"I said is that her, Pate?" she asked louder.

"Yeah, yeah, it's her now 'gone!'"

"I'm goin'! I'm goin'! Tell her I said hi, but matter fact…" Janie jumped out from behind the tree stump and ran pass a shouting Paton. In the back of his mind, knew that she would do something to embarrass him. Meeting Rain was that one thing.

Paton slowly eased off of the brick wall feeling the overwhelming need to beat Janie to Rain, but he kept himself level headed as he sort of cracked a smile at Janie's dash down the road. In a way, he wanted Janie and Rain to meet, being that she was the closest to him. Although he really didn't need her advice as far as manly items, he did need her for support, especially if everyone in Rain's family later turned against him after he'd possibly fallen in love.

Paton began to walk forward as Janie stopped in front of Rain, and he watched as Janie leaned in and gave her a light, friendly hug. After that, Janie turned toward him and tossed her arm around Rain like they had been friends forever. Then, she started to point her finger at Paton while running her mouth so much that Paton, instead of walking slowly, sped over to stop her from spilling too much more of his business.

"Hi, how you doin', Rain?" he asked her, while amazed at how she looked just as beautiful as the other day. Then he looked at Janie who stood right beside her causing him to chuckle when he thought to himself that Janie may be making her look even better than ever. "You look nice there in your pink dress. This here my nosey sister Janie. She just had to see you for herself…"

"'Course I did. Had to see what woman got my brother, that I loves so much, wantin' to marry…"

"Janie!" Paton shouted, causing Rain to burst into laughter. It was too late. Rain had heard everything, especially that word marry. It's the one thing she'd wanted for a while.

Janie jumped away from Rain quickly and slid over toward Paton's ear. "I know what a woman want, and all of us want that man to marry one day," she whispered, glanced back over her shoulder at a bashful Rain, and ran off. "Bye now, y'all!"

"It's nice to meet you!" Rain called after her as she waved her hand. Paton then walked up to her while her hand was still in the air, placed his hand on hers and brought it down to his side, and they walked together down the street.

"So where's the house your sister told me about?"

He shook his head and smiled as he continued to watch Janie as she made a detour from heading home to stop and talk to a man she knew at the corner store. "So Janie told you about a house, huh?"

"Yeah, she did. Told me you was fixin' it up. Say you a really good handy man."

"What else she tell you about me?"

"That was all until you cut her off. You gonna take me to see it?"

"Oh no," Paton stressed, ashamed that the house wasn't in the shape that it could be in. He appreciated Janie trying to make him look good in the eyes of Rain, but he didn't want her to know about the house until it was completely ready. "I'm not finished fixin' up the place how I want it, so…"

"Where do you live now?"

"I stay…my folks dead. Died a long time ago, so me and my sister there stay together in the house that was left to us." Then he looked back into her eyes. "I just now believe I found me a reason to leave into my own house."

"What reason is that?"

"Ain't a what. It's who."

"If you talkin' 'bout me, Paton," she responded as she paused mid stride, "you don't even know a thing about me and…"

"I know you like peach pie, picnics, and I even think you like me. Everything else, I'll learn in time 'cause all I got is as much time as you give me, Rain. How much time you plan on givin' me to learn 'bout you?"

Rain remained quiet as she started walking again, but Paton stayed put, holding on to her hand at the same time while watching her walk away. When she felt a slight tug on her wrist, she looked back at Paton who stood there waiting on a reply.

"Ain't you gonna answer me?"

"Answer what, Paton?" she asked, pretending to not have heard his question the first time, and that was when he gently pulled her back in front of him.

"I asked you how much time you plan on givin' me to learn what you feel like I need to know 'bout you, Rain, and I guarantee you I will learn whatever you need for me to know in that much time, even without you tellin' me a thing." He paused, and then continued. "So how much time you gonna give to me?"

"Take me where I wanna go, and I'll give you as much time as you ask me for."

"You mean to the house?"

"That's what I mean," she laughed. "I wanna see it."

Paton took a very deep breath and then let it all out. It was at that particular point that he didn't know what to do, but immediately, his deceased father's words conjured up inside him. He'd never wanted to disappoint him, not even while he laid in his grave, so he put on a strong demeanor though he felt otherwise and responded, "Okay, I'll take you there. It's not yet done, but I'll take you."

"Let's go, but your dress might get dirty. We have to go through a path back there in those trees. You trust me? Like I told you before, I won't hurt you none. You got my word."

"Yeah," she smiled. "Go 'head and take me. I'll follow you. I just need to be back here by three o'clock sharp."

"When we get to the worst part, and you think you gettin' too dirty, I'll carry you the rest of the way. How 'bout that?"

She nodded, and they headed off, and as they passed by Janie, she cut her eyes their way, failing to follow behind because she'd tucked a small bottle of liquor under her arm, courtesy of the gentleman who stood before her.

When they reached the old, rundown house that Paton planned to make into a home, he took the nice shirt that he wore off so that only his T-shirt would welcome the dirt and grime that covered certain areas. He watched as Rain looked around at the yard as well as the structure, and then she began to walk up the porch steps where he was.

"Wait, where you goin'?" Paton questioned her quickly, holding his hand out to stop her from coming any further. "It's not safe on these floors here. Got a whole bunch goin' on in here, Rain, and I don't want you to get..."

"I wanna go inside. Lemme see. I won't get hurt. Besides, that's what I got you for, ain't that right, Paton?" she flirted, this time, grabbing his hand, and Paton allowed her to lead him inside only a small distance before he took the lead. From there, he showed her the three bedroom home, the kitchen and what should be the small living area.

"It's small, but I'm gonna work on it as hard as I can, really hard." He excitedly explained. "Come here, and watch your step there...gimme those pretty hands. I wanna show you something at the back, probably the prettiest thing out here yet." He maneuvered Rain around some large nails and screws in the middle of the short hallway and into what he planned to make into the master bedroom. "Now, close your eyes, Rain."

"What?"

"Just close 'em for me. I promise you gon' be just fine. The only thing prettier than what I'm 'bout to show you is you." She closed her eyes, and afterward, Paton placed her in front of of the window and put his left hand over her eyes before speaking. "Long 'fore my mama and daddy died, she and my pops would come out here together, and each time, she would plant a bush or a tree. Now, at the time, I didn't know what she was plantin', but now…" he continued, removing his hand from the front of her eyes, "I see she was busy plantin' a beautiful future for us, her family... before things went wrong."

Beneath the silver, Spanish moss that hung down from the tall trees were the colors of Azaleas, Hydrangeas, and Trumpet flowers circling two bold Dogwood trees. There were so many colors that it looked like a whole different world at the back of the house than at the front. Paton backed away by a couple of steps and watched Rain's expression as she became amazed at the floral garden.

"Wow, Paton, this is beautiful!" She turned around to face him, and before he answered, she'd already turned back to look at the spectacle from the completely paneless window. "Your mom did this?"

"Janie takes care of it now I think 'cept she don't tell me she comes round here. I know she does, though. Who else is taking care of it but God Himself?" Paton continued to stare at her, confounded by how she made him feel about everything around him, like everything was becoming brand new again. Then, he walked over beside her. "I told you I could get you any type of flower you needed the other day, and here's my proof," he reminded her softly in her ear. Then, he moved her hair back a little more from her face as he adored her even more. "Your favorite color's pink. Am I right?"

"Yes. How'd you know?"

"Last time I saw you, you had a pink pocketbook and now you have on this nice pink dress, and your eyes keep movin' over there to those pink flowers at the corner." Glossing his eyes over her entire body as if she was a statuesque beauty, Rain began to feel a bit intimidated by the way he stared at her, so she started to move away. Paton didn't allow her to do so that easily as he only lightly touched the tips of her fingers with his, and continued to speak, his voice keeping her in position. "I notice everything about you, Rain."

As he spoke, he moved in closer, his lips met hers, and he kissed her passionately. Overtaken with an insatiable amount of emotion that he'd never had while with a woman, he touched her like she was as delicate as one of the flowers that sat directly outside the window. While kissing her, he smelled the radiance of her scent which became more precious to him than anything he'd ever smelled before. Just as he was about to pull away from her, afraid that he might have become too entangled with her in every way, she insisted that he stay by allowing her hands to stroll up his chest as her hands connected with each ripple of muscle formed beneath his brown skin. Finally, he placed both his hands around her waist as they continued to draw from each other's passion, lifted her from her stance, and placed her onto the open window's sill. Paton's arms became her shield from tumbling to the ground as he caressed her with care with his lips, from her neck to the tops of her breasts, and as his lips moved to massage her on the way back up to her lips, Rain became subdued by it all as a light wind drifted across her naked back while her dress began to move with Paton's hand up her spine. In an instant, their passion was silenced.

"Paton!" a voice called frantically some distance from the house. "Paton, hurry!"

Immediately, Paton stared into Rain's eyes and lifted her from the window sill apologetically, "I'm sorry if I…"

"No, no…" Before she could respond fully, she turned to the hallway as they both continued to hear an awful scream coming closer and closer. Finally, Paton walked over toward the hallway and noticed that it was the voice of his sister.

A look of desperation covered his face as he held out his hand to Rain who quickly ran over to him as he led her out of the house as fast as his feet could carry him. When he reached the porch, there was still no sign of Janie, which forced him into fearing the worst, so he called out as powerfully as he could, "Janie!" When he got no answer, he called again, and this time louder than previously. "Janie, where are you!"

"Paton, look," Rain interrupted, tugging at his arm, and when he turned to the right, his sister came barreling as fast as lightening through the woods. Paton ran over to her as Rain followed, just as concerned as Paton was about the screams.

"Paton, you gots to come on here now! It's Jesse, Paton." She glanced at Rain and then back into her brother's concerned face. "He been drinkin' like a wino and hollerin' like a hate filled crazy man, Pate…talkin' all kinda stuff… 'bout some fire and…"

Without any questions asked, Paton grabbed Rain's hand and raced forward, only stopping after remembering that he had to send Rain off in one piece. Therefore, he couldn't go back through the woods the same way Janie came.

"Janie, I got to get Rain back the other way, and I'll meet you up the road."

"Well, he out there outside Mr. Tallon's place, and Mr. Tallon can't do nothin' with him…scared he gone get put away if the police come, so we got to hurry on back."

Paton was already on the way as he heard his sister's words echo behind him. Rain was careful to follow Paton's steps as closely as possible while he moved like a man with tunnel vision through the debris filled trail. When they finally reached the end of the trail, he turned to face Rain as thoughts of his past sins came back to haunt him.

"Rain, I need to go and save a good friend of mine, and …"

"I'll come. My ride won't be here for a long time…"

"I really don't need…"

"Come on, Paton!" Janie screamed from the other side of the road where they said they would meet. "We got to go!"

Rain took two steps away from him as she watched Janie run down the road, and when Paton saw the unsettled and untrusting appearance of Rain's eyes, he feared losing what he thought was the woman he was supposed to be with for the rest of his life. Therefore, he took her by the hand and ran with her following closely behind while the only thing left to fog his mind was the day he avenged his close friend.

Approaching Mr. Tallon's place of business, Paton could already hear the screams and yells coming from what sounded like inside the store, however, when he got to the location, he found that the commotion was coming from the side. There was a man and a woman trying to contain the nearly six feet seven inches tall Jesse, but when Paton came around the corner, all the fighting ceased for only seconds.

Paton let loose of Rain's hand and moved her backwards as Janie stood there shouting at her brother to do something. As Paton stood there, Jesse stood staring right back at him, just like the day they stared at each other as the house fire burned those two men to death. It was obvious that Jesse had been drinking heavily. His body was leaned over, and he was out of breath from struggling with those who were not only trying to hold him but listening to every word that came from his mouth.

"Look who done showed up!"

Immediately, Paton rushed toward him, and the others let Jesse go as he stumbled forward into Paton's arms. "Jesse, man, listen here. You done had too much to drink there. It's time to go, friend. Time to go," Paton stated, noticing all the eyes on him, causing him to wonder why they were staring. As he stood Jesse up taller and more dignified, he continued to speak as Jesse only stared him in his face with a half cocked grin. "What you out here talkin' 'bout, Jess? Come on. Time to go back home."

Jesse then leaned in to his old friend's ear and strained a whisper, "You a killer, Paton." Jesse's eyeballs began to roll around at the onlookers, and then they land on the woman whom Paton brought along by his side – Rain. "You know who this here is, young fine thang? This here is Paton. He the man who set things a fire, ain't…"

"And ain't nothing left to say, Jesse!" he retorted as he gripped Jesse's neck and threw him onto the ground in front of everyone. He then jumped on top of him and squeezed Jesse's jaws together as his old friend stared back in horror. "You got something else to say to her, huh? Don't you never address her like that again. Now what you gone do is get yo' ass up," he continued under his breath as everyone stood back and watched, "and you gonna get on home 'fore the police come lookin'."

"You 'dey gone come a lookin' for, Pate, huh? For you or for me, huh, there, Paton?" he responded, completely drunk and suffering from a long time depression.

"Get up, Jesse, and gone on home. Janie," he called his sister and she ran over to him, kneeling right down beside him. "Take Rain on back to the house and tell her I'll be there. I got to get Jesse on down the road. You do that for me?"

She nodded her head and nervously walked over to Rain who was standing there looking confused and frustrated about what was going on with not only Paton, but the man he wrestled with on the ground.

"What's going on, Janie?" she asked, more concerned than ever.

"It ain't nothin', Rain. Listen here. Paton want you to come on back to the house, our house, with me 'til he get there. That's his old friend…they grew up together, and it seems that only Paton can only get him to settle down 'fore he get himself in trouble. This happen every so often with Jesse. He live right round the way, so come with me, and Paton gonna meet us back home fast as he can, okay?"

"You sure?" she asked, looking back at Paton for a response. Paton noticed her, and he nodded for her to go with Janie on back.

"See there. I told you. We just don't want him to get in more trouble than all that drinkin' will lead him to is all. Paton always lookin' after him."

"What about some fire…what he was sayin' about a fire?"

"I don't even know, girl. That's the wine be talkin'. I heard him say that one other time before, and don't nobody know what he talkin' 'bout 'til this day."

"Not even Paton?"

Janie looked back at her brother who was busy carrying Jesse back to his house as Jesse leaned on his shoulder. Then she turned back around and stared straight down the road. "No…not even my brother."

"It ain't never gone be alright, Paton. This here ain't never gone be right, not long as I'm livin'. They gone get us one day…"

"Get us for what?" Paton shouted on Jesse's front porch. "For what, huh?" Then he snatched the cup from Jesse's hand and threw it as hard as he could. "You need to let it go!"

"I can't sleep at night. Never could since Drowning Boy died. I ain't never got good dreams when I close my eyes…" Jesse wept. "I was tryin' to forget like my momma say…"

"And that's why I had to do what I did, Jesse, man! I had to. I ain't better than you. I couldn't hold it in. The same way I promised Drowning Boy, I done made that same promise to you. You gone be fine, but I ain't goin' to jail when it shoulda' been them in prison. I just let it burn."

89

"No we did! I did right long with you, and I shouldn'ta! I shouldn'ta. I ain't no killer," he cried. "I should'a tried to save 'em!"

There was a long silence between the two friends who share a common secret, until Paton spoke, "I'm not a killer either. Sometimes, I just do what I have to do to survive my own self," he stressed, jabbing his finger at his heart. "So, I done asked God to forgive me for my mama's sake and my own, but for my daddy's sake, I got to stay strong. That's all I know...and 'fore I let anybody, and I mean anybody alive, wear me thin 'til I can't make it no more, I'll hurt them more than they hurt me. God forgive me, but I will. Them white men, they hurt me, but I kill them just like they did Drowning Boy. I'd do it again. Not 'cause I wanted to, but because that's the only way I can see straight...knowin' that I got 'em back."

"And that ain't never gone be right, Paton. It's gone destroy you, Paton," Jesse's sick mother said through the window, causing Paton to shudder. "You mark my words, Paton. You gots to let people get off with murder sometimes in order to set yourself free, son. I knows whatcha did. I ain't tellin'. Tellin' on you will be like tellin' on my own. Gone 'way from Jesse now. Mark my words, evil for evil ain't the way. Leave that there anger to the devil or he gone take your mind from ya'. It ain't people you gots to worry 'bout, son. Thank you for bringin' Jesse back home, but now you 'gone off my property 'cause you sicker than he is. Just don't know it yet."

"And how you figure that?" Paton questioned her.

" 'Cause he can't live with that evil he let happen, but you can. You justifies it. Anytime you can justifies evil you done and live with it like it never happened, you got somethin' sick inside you. Real sick."

At that, Paton glanced back at Jesse and wandered off back to his own house, left to fix his thoughts and attitude for a possibly concerned Rain. By the time he got back to the house, he'd already masked the anxiety and fear brought on by, not only Jesse, but Jesse's slowly dying mother. There was a superstition that spoke volumes to Paton as he pretended to not be bothered by the words he heard come from the window of Jesse's house. The superstition was that whatever a sick, dying or old woman said from her mouth was always the truth, no matter how much it made no sense. It was an omen and bound to come true.

Janie went running out of the door to meet him as she watched him walk down the road toward the house while Rain exited the front screen door and waited. Paton's eyes stared beyond his sister, who ended up stumbling over a stick, and concentrated on Rain. He was trying to detect her mood from afar, wanting to prepare himself for the worst. He knew it hadn't been any more than thirty minutes that he'd been apart from Rain, but the thought plagued him that she might be uninterested since seeing what happened back at the store.

"So what happened back there, Pate? You got him home good? Ain't no police came, ain't it?"

"No, Janie. Nothin' like that. How's Rain? She alright?"

"I said is Jesse back home?" Janie stressed.

"Yeah, now calm down. You gave her somethin' to eat."

"Yeah, I did. She's nice, too. Ain't try to mind your business neither. I told her 'bout Jesse though, and how he drinkin' and talkin'…it don't mix. She asked about the fire…"

Paton stopped in his tracks again and stared at Janie as if he didn't even know her. The only person he thought even knew about that fire was his dead mom before he found out Jesse's mom also knew. The last person he wanted to know was his sister.

"Fire?" Paton responded, shoving it to the back of his mind so that he could make it another day without going crazy.

"Yeah, he was ramblin' 'bout a fire again."

"Ain't nothing." Paton started walking toward the house once more. "He always saying that when he get drunk."

"He always got your name in it though…"

Paton stopped in his tracks, and Janie could tell she'd hit a nerve. She'd always known the sweetness of her brother, but she'd also never wanted to see him angry if she could help it. It was something that she couldn't handle. Instead of losing control, he stared at Rain. It was Rain that kept him settled enough to walk back to the house, not responding to anything else Janie said.

As he walked up the porch, Janie passed them both to go back inside the house. Rain just stood there, and her eyes asked the question of what happened. Paton read them as if he'd known her for a lifetime. When he sat down on the porch's step, he looked up at her, and she came down to sit next to him.

"I'm sorry about all that down at the store. He was my friend."

"Was?"

"We grew up together. Been through a bunch," he sighed as he looked around at the yard that he played in as a boy. "He was with me when a friend of ours got shot down. We was playin' a joke, wasn't nothin' big, but we didn't know we was on some bought land when…"

"They shot him down. I remember my mama talkin' about it. It was all around this side… I remember because it shook my poppa so bad that he didn't let me go nowhere. They say it was a big boy…"

"Drowning Boy," Paton interjected. "Now Jesse gone a lil crazy is all. He tried to hold it all in…" Paton reached over and grabbed her hand. "I don't wanna hold nothin' in. I'm not like that. When I got mad, he got quiet. It ran him crazy. Everything alright now though," he smiled. "You alright?"

"Yeah, I'm alright. Sorry about your friend." She leaned her head on his shoulder, and from that day, they began seeing each other more and more.

Every Saturday, Rain would come over, and even meet him at the house he was working on every hour that he could. Paton would take her places, places she'd never been before, and have her back home safely before dark with a full stomach. He tried to prove every waking minute that he loved her from the very first time he saw her, and she began to believe it. Not only that, she fell deeply in love with him as well.

"I want you to meet him now. I'm tired of hiding you out. My poppa already asked about you, but I told him you work so hard…but this weekend here, you would take off to come by."

"You told him what?" Paton asked, wiping his mouth from the fresh biscuits his sister made for him as they both sat on the newly sanded floor in what was looking to be a fine house for those two to settle in.

"I told him that when I came home today that you would be with me."

"Rain, you see how I look?"

"All the better, Paton. My father respects a man who works hard and can take care of me like you been doing. I love you, so I think that he should meet you, clean or not. 'Sides that, we can go home and take a bath…"

"We can?" he kidded, taking a bite of his apple.

"Not us, Paton, stop playin'!"

"Well that's what you said…us. I thought…"

"Well, stop thinkin'. Let me think. You just listen."

"Lean over here and give me kiss. I ain't got to listen to nothin' else. No need in convincin' me. I'll go where you want me to go, meet who you want me to meet. I was just waitin' on you to ask me anyhow."

"You were?" Rain stated, getting up from the floor.

"Yeah. You ready?" he asked as he followed her up off the floor. Noticing her hesitation, he asked her once again. "You sho' you ready? I see you lookin' around here at this place like you never been here before."

"You really did all this for me?"

"I did it all for our family. The one I want with you. That's the reason I did it. Ain't another woman in the world worth all this but you. Even if your daddy don't let you come with me, Rain," he paused and then kissed her on the cheek. "You comin' with me anyhow. This your house."

"And we gonna get married!" she squealed, jumping on his neck and squeezing it so tightly that he nearly choked on the food that he hadn't fully swallowed. "And Paton, we don't even need a full weddin'. I just wanna get married is all. That's all I want."

"You askin'?" Paton joked, then she moved from his neck and stepped back by about three full steps. Then she held out her hand.

"Paton?"

"Yes ma'am," he responded, standing tall like a soldier.

"I want you to marry me. When you gonna get me a ring for this finger?" she asked, wiggling the fingers of her left hand wildly.

Paton moved closer to her and took her by the hand. As he brought her into his space, he gave her a nice kiss on the lips, and as he kissed her, he slid something onto her ring finger slowly. Rain was so caught up in his passionate kiss that she only thought he was caressing her hand as he normally did every time they were together.

After Paton secretly slid the ring on her finger, he kept holding her hand as he stepped back and lowered himself to one knee. Rain continued believing that his kneeling was all a part of her game while Paton kept her left hand fully covered by both of his. Then, he finally proposed, "Rain, will you marry me?"

"Yes, I will, Paton Jones. I'll be glad to be your wife and have our kids and…" she answered, but stopped talking as he removed his hands from hers, revealing the ring he gently placed on her finger. "Oh sweet, Jesus!" she panted as her eyes lit up with excitement.

"My name's Paton, baby girl. I ain't Jesus."

"Oh Jesus, yes! Yes, I'm gonna marry you, and you better not ask another woman on this earth either!" she yelled, falling on top of him causing him to lose his balance and hit the floor. Before Paton could even get a word out, she'd already planted her lips on his and repeated their future names over and over again – Mr. and Mrs. Paton and Rain Jones.

THE MONSTER

"Paton! Wake up! Wake up!" Janie screamed from Paton's room door. It was in the middle of the night, nearing two o'clock in the morning, and Paton was trembling and fighting all at the same time as he struggled to open his eyes and awaken from his terrible nightmare. He hadn't had nightmares for one whole year which was beyond normal making this particular night a scary one. Ever since Drowning Boy, his mother and father died, the nightmares he'd had since he was a teen increased, turning Paton into someone else when he was left alone to deal with his own feelings. Something that Janie didn't know about had triggered them back again, and she didn't know where to turn for help because Paton never wanted any help. He never wanted anybody to know, so the family always kept his other side a secret as much as possible.

"Paton, I say wake up!" Shivering in the chills of fear on a warm summer night, she ran to pick up the bat that she kept near the front door. More terrified than she'd ever been while living with her brother whom she loved so much, she was prepared to knock his knees in if he came after her like he'd done in a crazed fit before. Tears started to fall from Janie's eyes as she walked back toward her brother's room cautiously, her wrists shaking out of fear of the unknown. "Paton, it's me Janie. You havin' another nightmare like you done had the other night. Now either go back to sleep or…" Before the rest of her words got out, there stood Paton at his room door, his eyes bloodshot while the breath came through his nostrils like madman. His head was cocked up high while his eyes slanted down directly at his sister's face as if he could take her life at any moment.

He just stood there like a wild animal waiting on any type of fresh movement that would cause him to attack, but after one minute of a horrifyingly tense stare down, Paton retreated, crawled back into his bed and went to sleep as if nothing ever happened. Janie continued to stand there in the hallway, scared to death of moving at all past his room door as the urine ran down her legs. She slept there until the morning, afraid to wake what she'd started to call the dead. The next morning, she woke up, washed and started drinking and cooking to get her nerves in order before Paton got up.

As she stood over the stove, she tapped her foot like a woman with much on her mind. That was when she heard Paton stirring around in his room. She threw her small liquor bottle underneath the sink and started making him some lunch before he set out to work. When Paton came around the corner, she tossed his lunch on the table and folded her arms, glaring at her brother while waiting on an apology.

"You got to stop this here stuff, Paton. I'm sick of it. You done scared me half to death again…thought you was gonna attack me like…"

"Like what, Janie? Like what?" As he shouted back at her, he hauled off and threw his shoe against the wall. "I don't remember nothing. Only reason I know I had a nightmare was because I saw you 'fore I got back in the bed," he shouted, nearly in tears before he hung his head low, turning his eyes in shame away from his sister. "I ain't know it was you, Janie. When I come awake, I was standing there lookin' at you, but I thought you was somebody else for a minute."

Janie rushed beside him, grabbed a chair and took a seat at the table. "Listen here. You 'bout to be married in two weeks, Paton, and…"

"You think I don't know that?"

"Well you need to tell her 'bout yourself at night! You be done scare that chile breasts to her back on your honeymoon night, Pate," she stressed. "What got you so riled up that them dreams keep turning you into some monster? I thought you was over them things, and here they are right back again."

"I don't know," he answered in a low tone. "And don't worry 'bout me and Rain none. I'll be more occupied with her in our house, and my mind won't have no time to…"

"Go crazy on her?"

"No, Janie. I won't have no time to be alone no more." A tear came down his eye, and Janie reached over to wipe it but he stopped her hand mid air. "Don't you tell nobody. Don't tell nobody nothing 'bout me, that I go numb and dumb at night. I just want somebody to love and who love me back. I need to be back like I used to be. Sometimes I don't even know myself…but when I'm with her, I can breathe."

"Paton, you might need some kinda help with all you carrying. It's been so long, and you seem to be gettin' worse…"

"I ain't gettin' worse, Janie," he pleaded. "Now please, let me 'lone about it. I wanna get married to Rain. She real good to me, and she want a family. It'll keep my mind off everything. Just got a lot going on right now, but when I'm married and everything die down, I'ma be back to

where even our own mama would want me…at peace." He
grabbed her hand. "I'm sorry for scaring you so much. I
love you, sis."

Hesitantly, Janie agreed with him, "Alright then."
She looked down at the floor nervously, and then, left the
seat to walk back over to the counter. "You better eat and get
to work." With a forced smile, she turned back around to
look at him once again. "Because you 'bout to be a married
man, Mr. Paton Jones, and I'm 'bout to have another sister!
Ha! I love you, too." When she turned back around to slice
some cheese, her smile turned south. She was worried about
the constant denial that her brother was in about his mental
health. Still, she loved her brother like she loved her own
self, and if hiding his secret was that important to him to feel
like a complete man, then she would.

After Paton finished eating, he got his things and left.
She watched him walk out the door, not taking her eyes off
of him. Before getting herself ready to go to work, she
reached back underneath the counter and took another drink
of her liquor, and each night up until the day before the
wedding, she continued to drink to settle her nerves. The
night before the wedding, she and her brother spent one last
night in the same house while sitting on the porch with a
picture of their parents in their hands.

"Mama and daddy are looking down from heaven
right now at they big boy, and they proud. You gettin'
married!" She pinched his cheeks, and he pulled away in
laughter. "You ain't nervous?"

"No, no I ain't nervous. I just don't wanna mess
things up. I done saved up some money, working good, and I
got everything I'm supposed to have 'fore I start a family,
ain't it? Just wanna have somethin' go right in my life and
not wrong."

"Look here. Don't you think nothin' 'bout all that. Let me handle them troubles of the past. You gone on and live your life, and all that bad stuff will stay right here inside me 'til the day I die. You 'gone be fine. Matter fact," she continued, getting up from her seat to walk back into the house, "I'll be right back."

"Where you goin'?"

"Just wait a minute."

He heard the screen door shut behind him, and then he looked up at the night sky. The big dipper seemed to always be located over his house, and he would always imagine it empty, with only drops of water here and there inside of it. That night though, when he looked up at the formation of those same stars, he saw the dipper as completely full of promise, and it was finally ready to pour all of what was inside of it out. Paton was ready for that to happen because all his memories were clouded by pain and misery. He was ready to catch what everyone else around him was catching, just a piece of goodness from heaven. Just a small piece of blessings would make things alright for Paton, and he knew deep down in his heart that Rain was the beginning of what he would call his new life.

Disrupting his gaze into the stars, Janie came out of the house holding something at her side. Paton noticed, but he didn't say anything, waiting on her to do the talking. When she didn't, he waited only about thirty seconds longer and then asked, "Janie, what?"

From behind her back, she pulled out a small bottle of liquor, the same kind she drinks to calm her nerves. "This is something that you may want to keep you calm while you're with her, you know…just in case you get pulled outta yourself and violent like you do when you…"

"You givin' me some gin, Janie?" he asked disgusted. "I don't do no drinkin'." He stood up. "Man, Janie, I'm 'bout to get married, and I got enough problems to deal with…"

"Just take it in case." Janie desperately stood to her feet and grabbed Paton by the arm. "Paton, I ain't gone be there to hold you down or hold you back! This here I'm givin' you ain't to make you sicker, but this here all I know to keep my pain inside. It been workin'. Here."

She reached over and placed the small bottle into Paton's hand, and Paton slowly wrapped his fingers around it. "What mama told me to do been workin'. I go be by myself and try to pray it off."

"But what if your mind go before then? What if you can't pray?"

"I'ma be fine. I'll let my wife take care of me at that time, Janie. You can take this here bottle back. Don't be givin' me your problems as no gift." He stared Janie down in disbelief, dropped the bottle at her feet, and went back inside, not angry at her, but understanding that she only wanted him to be okay. That was the only way she knew how to be alright with things, so that was her answer to him. Paton decided to keep praying and being strong just like he was taught to do, and soon enough, he believed those demons would leave really soon and never come back. Besides, it was time to get married.

The wedding took place outside the home he renovated where Paton waited for his bride to come around the corner. He, Tunk and Rain's father cleaned and cleared up the yard that, when finished, turned into a colorful floral garden. There was something extra special about choosing the place that his mother and father made plans for because it felt to him that his parents were in attendance. Having a small ceremony there was Rain's idea. After she learned how precious and caring Paton's mom was, she felt it only fitting to be married in a garden she planted with her own hands. It was done with love, and Rain knew it would be a great gift to her future husband to have his mother there alive in the flowers.

As Paton stood there anticipating Rain coming around the corner in a beautiful dress, he glanced over at Janie who'd already taken her place next to Rain's mother who was smiling with glee, staring at the surroundings and waiting on her daughter to come out with her father. Even January, Paton's eldest sister who had moved a long time ago and married when he was a little boy, came back down to see her brother marry off just for one day. It was Paton's first time even seeing Rain's older sister May who attended the wedding. They looked just alike except May had her by years.

No one bought anything brand new because although everyone saved money, times were still hard, and no one had extra money to spare on fancy attire. Therefore, they wore the best they already had with a couple extras. As far as money was concerned, people brought what they had and stuffed it in a hole at the porch.

The preacher from the church was already there in his suit, and if it wasn't for the cascading trees, he would have burned up along with the rest of the men in their suits because it was a smoldering hot day. Even the rain strained to fall from the sky as a result of the blazing sun after it had smelled like rain was on the way for hours.

Paton turned to the side as Tunk wiped sweat from his face, and as soon as he faced forward again, there she was in her father's arm. Rain wore a white dress which Paton believed she made beautiful even though it was a dated dress, belonging to her mother at the time of her wedding. As she walked the short aisle with her proud and serious father, Paton stared into her eyes while she stared back into his. Although everyone that they cared for was around, the only person Paton saw at that time was her. Rain was his only concern and would be for the rest of his life. That was the promise that he would make to God as he stood there with his brown suit on and his father's dress shoes with every witness he could have on earth and in heaven. Finally, his bride met him at the altar of flowers, and it was the very first time that he allowed a tear to flow down his face in front of her, enraptured by his love for her.

As the preacher spoke the words of the scripture and of love, Paton didn't listen. Rain consumed him as if she were his only source of freedom and passion. Although she wore the color white, they'd already secretly made love half a dozen times in the year that had gone by, untamed and full of desire for one another. The last time their bodies had come together in heated passion was twenty whole days ago, and Paton couldn't wait to have her in his arms once again, except this time, it would be until they parted ways at death. For Paton, he hoped it would be a very long time until then.

When it was time for Paton to have his bride, he kissed her slowly and passionately while everyone adored what looked to be true love. Rain's parents looked on exceptionally happy for the union, and Tunk had a big smile on his face while nodding his head in agreement. Finally, Janie moved forward with the broom, placed it on the ground, and Paton and Rain jumped over it hand in hand as husband and wife. Then, their honeymoon began in their home.

<u>Two Months Later</u>

"You feelin' alright there, baby girl?" Paton asked as he voluntarily moved her plate from the table. She'd barely eaten any food, and he noticed that her face was full of worry since he'd gotten home from work. "Come here," he said, taking her hand, not wanting her to get up from her seat. Instead, he moved back toward her, kneeled down, and continued speaking. "How long you been feelin' bad? I can tell since I came through the door."

Rain uneasily answered him, shifting her eyes to the floor. "I'm alright, Paton. Maybe I'm just tired. I mean I have been working, but not hard. Just three days a week, but..."

"Well maybe you need to stop all that workin'. I makes enough money for us, and I don't plan on stoppin'. I ain't one to keep you stuffed up in this house by yourself all day. You know I want you to keep on livin' and doing the things you like to do, but I want you to be feelin' good at the same time. If you can't do that, I need you to stop workin', Rain. What good am I to you if I can't put a smile on your face?"

Rain stood up in front of him, resulting in Paton standing up with her. "You right, Paton. I think I might take a break on things for maybe a week or so, then I can get back to doing what I was doing. I must be coming down with somethin' real bad," she answered, not looking him in his eyes. Instead, she pushed away from him, sliding by his presence. Paton reacted by reaching for her hand. She then turned around with watery eyes.

"Rain," he called concerned. "What's the matter? I do something? You in pain? Come on and lay down. Lemme go get your mama…"

"No, Paton. It's nothin'. I just need to lay down. Will you get me some warm water and a cloth for my head?" she asked weakly to a husband who didn't know what to do.

"Okay, but lemme help you in the bed. Why ain't you tell me you wasn't feeling good today? I'da never left you," he assured her, picking her up and carrying her to their neatly made bed. The window was up and the fresh smell of flowers came flowing inside as he laid her down. He took her shoes off of her feet and rushed to get her just what she'd asked for. By the time he got back, Rain's eyes were closed, and she was fast asleep. Instead of going outside as he normally would after dinner to sit on the porch, he pulled a chair up next to Rain as she lay there, and made sure she was fine all night. He didn't plan on leaving her for work the next day, and he kept to his plans.

The very next morning after barely sleeping a wink and troubled by watching Rain barely move throughout the night, he went into the kitchen, chopped up some onions really fine like he remembered his mother doing for him when he got sick, boiled them in the pot and seasoned it with some black pepper. The point was to keep it on the stove steaming just in case whoever was sick needed it to breathe better, clear their chest of cold, or either drink it. It was what Paton's mom would call the food to go along with the prayer, and for him, it worked every time.

From there, Paton folded his hands over the food, bowed and prayed to the Lord Jesus that He heal Rain and allow the food to help her and not harm her. Right before they married, Rain bought some pure white bowls with a floral design. He reached for one and poured some of the soup inside it. Lightly blowing it on the way back to the bedroom, he walked inside to see Rain with her eyes opened partially. As he walked over to his chair, Rain leaped from the bed like a scared cat and raced to the bathroom. Paton sat the bowl down and followed her, but she slammed the door in his face before he could go inside. Then, he nervously waited outside the door.

"Rain? Rain, baby, you alright in there? If you don't answer me, I'm coming in."

"Yeah…" she struggled, but when Paton heard the sound of her vomiting, he felt helpless. When he turned the knob to open the door after about twenty seconds of standing impatiently, Rain placed her weight against it, silently refusing to let him inside. Finally, Paton whispered at the door. "Rain, I love you. Just let me in…I need to check on you," he pleaded, rubbing his forehead while glancing back at the front door, wondering if he should run off and get help. "Rain…" At his last call, the door opened, and Rain stood there at the sink, staring at her reflection in the mirror, and through that same mirror, she looked back at Paton. Her eyes were weak, and she breathed like she would faint if she didn't hold on as tight as she could to the edges of the counter.

When Paton placed one foot into the bathroom, she spoke. "I think I'm pregnant, Pate," she stated, as her hands fell to her side hopelessly, and she spoke again, this time with an even heavier heart. "I think I got a baby…" she stuttered, finally turning to stare directly at her husband like her world was falling apart.

Paton, as soon as he heard the news, wanted to feel happiness, however, with the tears beginning to fall down Rain's face, he embraced her. Rain's body went limp in

Paton's arms, and because she wouldn't stand anymore, he went down to his knees with her in his arms.

"Rain, it's a good thing, baby. Look at me, look right here," he commanded her by touching her face and moving her to stare right back at him. "You my wife," he strained, wiping the tears from her eyes and moving her hair away from her face. "Rain, there ain't nobody else in the world I wanna have a baby with but you. What you cryin' for, huh?"

Rain didn't answer quickly. She only examined how much he loved her, and as she sat there, he kissed her on her cheeks, got a wet rag and started to wipe her face. As he wiped her down, she reached for his hand. "It just scared me that's all. This is my first time…about to be a mom. I'm just scared…"

"Ain't nothing to be scared about. You ain't never got to be scared of nothing in your life long as you with me. Never, Rain." Then, he smiled. "If you sho' you pregnant, that mean I'm 'bout to be a daddy. Ain't that what that means, baby, that I'm 'bout to be the happiest daddy in all this town?"

Rain nodded her head as the tears continued to flow down her face. He then stood her to her feet, lifted her slowly from the ground and then took her back to bed. After that, he ran to the kitchen to get her a glass of milk. From there, he stripped down from the clothes he had on, ran to wash and then put on some shorts and a T-shirt all in less than fifteen minutes.

"Wait, Paton, where you goin'?"

"Rain, baby, I don't know how to take care of you," he responded with his hands in the air, smiling from ear to ear. "Ain't no onion soup gonna take care of what's goin' on here now. I got to go get your mama. Let her know she 'bout to be a grandma!"

"What?" Rain asked, beginning to get excited because of how she saw Paton running around the room, getting things cleaned up before he ran out.

"I said…" He ran over to her and gave her a big kiss on her lips. "Tossin' that onion soup over there out the door and going to get my baby's grandma. Ain't no way you workin' right now no mo'. I ain't gonna letcha. I'm gonna get your mama, and when she get you well, all you gonna need to do is sit back and relax until my baby get here," Paton said, tossing on his shoes and running to the door before stopping and turning back around. "Wait, Rain…you sho'? You absolutely sho' you pregnant?"

Rain giggled at the way Paton looked, like a fumbling, happy school boy that got his first girlfriend. "I could be wrong, but I don't think I am. I don't have a cold, but I'm sick all over, like I wanna keep eatin' but can't do it without…"

Paton didn't stick around to hear her say more. He yelled hallelujah all the way out the door along with other words that affirmed his happiness over becoming a father. As he ran down the path toward the street to catch a ride to his in-laws, he thought about how he lost his family and friend at such an early age. The thought that God was gonna give it all back to him in his own family, who would then become his best friends, was the best thing that Paton could ask for. He'd already stopped the nightmares and sleep walking since he'd been resting with Rain, and life could only get much better with a baby – his baby.

Once Rain's mother came to the house for one week, along with the help of a midwife's knowledge, Rain was back on her feet and feeling much better. Rain was assumed to have been suffering from low iron, nausea, and dehydration, so they gave her beet juice and other vegetables that would help lift not only her body back to normal, but also her spirits.

"Sometimes when a woman gets pregnant, Paton, things change inside her…something like when the flow come but in other ways. She's gonna be fine. Just keep makin' this here juice up like I tell you. Can't let no baby come in this world without the right food in the mama belly. Baby won't be right at all. I'll come 'round yonder once every two weeks until that baby get here, and if you need me, you know where I'll be, you here? Got me a garden, so come 'round after work and get some greens. You gonna need 'em, and I got plenty, plus I'll lend you a chicken or two. Eggs do her some good." The midwife walked to the door where her ride was waiting out front. "I'm gonna go by your mama church this evening, Rain, and ask her to show you how to sew. You gonna be gettin' big, and depending on how you carry that baby, you can either go wide or all in the front with your skinny self," she laughed. "Save you some money if you know how to make them clothes…might not be the same after." She kept talking and laughing as she got into the car and was driven away.

For the next months, Rain grew and grew. She grew so big from eating so much and the baby growing so much that she really couldn't fit any of her clothes at all. Rain's mother, Sunflower, already knitted plenty blankets for the child, but totally forgot about any clothes for her own daughter. She had exactly five brand new simple dresses that would do only for a while, but she needed five more. Still, she made due with what she had while Paton took care of the rest of what needed to be done in the house.

Besides cleaning the house where Rain couldn't because of her back pains that started coming on by the fifth month really badly, he would run her a warm bath every night to get her relaxed. After he washed her back and massaged her shoulders, he would gather up pillows on the bed so that when she got out of the bathroom, she could recline on the bed. Some nights, Paton even slept on the floor because he was overly concerned about making the mattress lean a particular way, resulting in Rain's back straining.

What made him even more paranoid was Rain's reflux. She was constantly having a problem with her food being kept down. That was when Mama Sunflower would bring him ginger root so he could make Rain some tea which was supposed to help her stomach. Most times it did, but there were some times where all he could do was make sure she didn't come down off those pillows he had propped up on the bed. Rain would be so tired sometimes from not being able to get a good night's rest that Paton would just come home from work and cook after demanding that she stayed in the bed. He didn't want her to lift a finger. From what he was told, a woman was at her closest to the grave when she was with a child inside of her, and this terrified him. He couldn't stomach losing her nor his child, not after losing nearly every other person in his life. Therefore, he did everything he could do.

Rain started reading the Bible more and more. She began to read it so much until it was all she did. Paton literally had to take it from her hands just to get her to eat her food. Something was bothering her, and he couldn't put his finger on it. Paton simply felt that it was what the midwife told him it was, the pregnancy making her act different, preparing for a baby and being a mom, wanting everything to be perfect before the arrival, including herself. In the back of his mind though, there was always a nagging thought that something else was bothering Rain. He just didn't have the heart to bother her about it, so he talked to Janie.

***

"I don't know what it is, Janie," he whispered. "Seem like she goes off into another world, ain't nothing like the Rain I met before."

"She back there sleepin'?" Janie asked, peeking inside the screen door.

"Yeah, she back there, so keep it down. I ain't meaning to tell her business, so don't go running your mouth. You just the only person I can tell about this. Can't tell Mama Sunflower because she just gonna start all that hummin' and won't give me an answer to nothin' I ask. Too busy thinkin' letting stuff alone will make it turn for the better. Janie," he paused, "I sure hope nothin' ain't wrong with her."

"Forget about her being moody, Pate, 'cause that's all it is – pregnancy blues is all. Just be glad she not rippin' your throat off. What about you though? You been…"

"I been fine, Janie," he dragged. "Just fine. Ain't had a nightmare since I left," he boasted. "Told ya'. All that stuff was gonna leave me alone once I got away from it and started to control everything around me." He went quiet and started to rub on a small pile of dirt that was on the wooden rail of the house. "I ain't gonna never lose control again of nothin' around me. I see what poppa meant now, and it feels good to have my own. My wife, my baby comin', my house…I even got money saved for near 'bout five years strong hidden in there."

"You gettin' old, Pate."

112

"You just as old as me. Hush yo' mouth, girl. So you think it's just her being pregnant?"

Janie turned to look directly at him with a straight face so that he would know she was serious. "It ain't nothing but the baby. That's all. Just the baby." Then, she squinted her eyes. "You done made love to her whiles she like that?"

"Girl, move, fo' I throw you off this porch. Put that bottle down, too. You don't need it. Becoming a habit for you, Janie. Make you say stupid stuff like you sayin' now."

"No it ain't," she snapped back. "I just drink it when I want to relax. Ain't nothin' wrong with that. Some of us ain't married, you know. I'm by myself in there," she stated in a whisper that Paton could barely hear as she turned to go down the steps of the porch.

"Where you going?"

"On home," she responded, unable to look into her brother's eyes. He didn't know it, but she'd gotten awfully lonely in the house all by herself, so much so that she yearned to have her brother back with her. Janie would be in the house at times, and in the middle of the night, she thought she would hear her deceased mom humming tunes in the kitchen. When she would go inside, there would be no one. This was what led her to drinking even more; it kept the noises away. "And you ain't got to walk me. I'll be fine. Catch a ride where I normally do...ain't nobody ever minded givin' me no ride." she said with her head down. "Or I can walk. It won't be sun down, Paton, before I get back."

"Well, hurry up, Janie. I mean it," he ordered her, deepening his tone as a revelation of his seriousness. Janie didn't answer him. All she did was throw her hand up in the air and wave good-bye. Paton stood where he was on the porch, watching her walk until he couldn't see her anymore.

Fact was, he wasn't about to walk her back that early, at least that was the plan. She was supposed to wait until Rain woke up, but Paton already knew that Janie was stubborn when she could be. All that known, Paton felt uneasy about letting her be alone that night. He could sense that something was wrong with Janie, and the more he tried to ignore it, the worse it felt.

***

"Rain, baby. How you feelin'?"

"I'm better. Can't stop sleepin'," she laughed. "This baby is workin' me already," she said as she grabbed a cup from the cabinet and proceeded to pour herself a glass of water. Paton, who stood behind her shirtless, placed his hand around her stomach and rubbed her pregnant belly. Then, he gave her a kiss on her neck.

"If you're feelin' okay, I have to run to check on Janie. She wasn't right when she left here..."

"She was here? I didn't know," she explained while gulping down the water from her cup.

"You were sleepin', but if you think you're gonna be alright for about thirty minutes to an hour, I need to go check on her."

"Somethin' the matter?"

"I just got this feelin' in my gut, and when I get that feelin', it ain't wrong, Rain. I just need to check on her." He reached back for his shirt that was hanging off of the chair.

As he pulled it down over his head, Rain leaned in and rubbed his chest and then kissed him on his chin.

"Go 'head. I'll be fine."

"I got the gun in the back…"

"Paton, ain't nobody 'round here to even come 'round here. It's just a bunch of woods and weeds in the front and my favorite flowers in the back," she exclaimed. "Just hurry up back here. 'Sides that, you know ain't no bullets in that gun," she laughed, causing him to laugh, too. "We need to get some though."

"Baby, just stay put. Don't answer the door. I don't need to knock. If it's a knock, it ain't me."

"Paton…" she sighed. "Bye now…"

"Take care of my baby."

"I'm not your baby no mo'?" Rain asked flirting a little, alerting Paton to the fact that she may be feeling a little better than she had been.

"You're gonna always be my baby." He kissed her and ran further and further away from his house only to get to his sister's house in twenty minutes. When he didn't see her room light or any other lights on in the house as the sun had already set, he panicked because his senses were just about screaming at him to hurry to the house.

Already out of breath, he still took off running up the porch steps and to the door, hoping to find a sleeping Janie in the room. Although he didn't live there anymore, he kept the key to get in. As he unlocked the door, he leaped inside the house with Janie's name on the top of his tongue.

"Janie!" At the sound of his voice, there was only the stillness of the house to return his call. He searched the house, first stopping at her room, and just like he felt, she wasn't there. "Janie, answer me!" His heart started to beat wildly as he rushed through the house like a warrior on the hunt for the enemy, believing that someone had attacked his sister on the way home. His mind started to become riddled with thoughts that provoked anger and loss, something that he hadn't learned to deal with since he was a child.

While his mind continued to conjure up thoughts based off of pure adrenaline and stress, his body began to release them, throwing blow after blow onto each wall he passed by. Every door, instead of being pushed open, was kicked and the floor stomped until he finally went out the side door where he paced to the back of the house. It was there where he found no sign of Janie either.

"Janie!" he hollered out so loudly that he felt the quake inside his stomach. He remembered that she said she was gonna go to the shop for a ride back to the house, so he went back inside, locked up the house, and started running once again. As he passed by the mailbox, he heard a voice coming from the grass. It was a female's voice, and it sounded like his sister crying.

Without hesitation, he ran toward where he thought the sound came from, and as he poked through the darkness, he saw a design in the grass that didn't match the normal pattern. The disruption was Janie, and she was sprawled out on the lawn, giggling and crying at the same time. When she noticed him coming closer, she began to ramble.

"You shoulda' seen yourself…coming running down that street," she laughed, "Fast, too. You was movin' like this," she explained as she demonstrated with her legs up in the air, pretending to run fast as she lie there on her back.

When she finished her demonstration, she allowed her legs to fall right back to the ground. Then, she lifted her drink to her mouth. "I tried to call you, but you was…gone," she sang. "You was gone down that road there. When you bust in the house, I figure you was gonna just lay down there and go on to sleep like you normally…"

Paton went down to the ground with her, relieved that he'd found her in one piece, but when he tried to pick her up, she snatched away.

"I ain't goin' back in there," she snarled like a wild woman. The look in her eyes was evil, and her expression was one of hatred. "Ain't nothin' in there for me but memories. Only reason I don't do what you do is 'cause I drinks. See this…" she said, twirling her bottle in his face. "I drinks. I won't have no dreams of mama no more with these bottles. Paton," she whispered as she lifted her finger to call him closer to her face. "She be in there. She be just a hummin' away when I go to sleep. Ever since you left…that's what she been…" Then, she looked toward the house. "Shh…you hear that?"

"Mama not in there, Janie. She gone. Been gone, and she ain't never hummed since, now get up."

"Why can't nobody fall in love with me?" she shouted. "I'm just as nice as your pretty lil' wife, ain't I? So why can't I get a man to marry me, huh, Paton? Tell me that, Pate. How come? Is I too ugly, black or po'…which one? I stink to death, huh, Paton? My tits don't sit up…" she continued, grabbing at herself until her brother slapped her hand down. Then she started laughing hysterically. It was then that Paton learned the most about his sister, so instead of him letting her sleep at her house, he made the decision to take her back home with himself and Rain for the night. She was living with a heart that had nothing left, and it was just like he felt before he met Rain. Janie would end up staying there on and off for months until Rain gave birth.

"Look at her, Paton," Rain gleamed over their new baby girl whom she rocked back and forth in her arms. "Just look at her, y'all! Mama, can you believe it? I'm a mama just like you," she laughed while her mom sat back and adored the newborn baby girl named Jocelyn.

"I believe it alright, chile," she laughed. "You just remember everything I taught you, and I'ma come 'round here with your daddy everyday next week while Paton gone to work so you can get some rest as I take care of lil Jocie."

"Jocie? That's what you gone call my baby, mama? Jocie?"

"Yes I am. Done already decided," she laughed as she got up to go to the front door before heading to the car. "See you later, son," she said as she passed by him while Paton opened the screen door to let her out.

"Alright, Mama Sunflower. See you real soon," he said, sending her off with an uneasy smile. There was something bothering him ever since Rain gave birth yesterday, and he still hadn't said anything about what was on his mind. The whole scene was terrible as far as Paton was concerned, to hear his wife screaming from the other room was enough to send him outside with his father in law. When he got there, he was still unable to shield his ears from all the commotion, so much so that he ran. Nobody understood why he ran, but he did. He ran all the way through the woods until he found the biggest tree he could find to hide behind. From there, he waited with his eyes closed, trying to blot out the visual of his mom nearly dying on that floor in a pool of blood when she gave birth the day Drowning Boy died along with his baby sister.

With every scream and moan Rain belted out, flashbacks rushed into Paton's memory, bombarding him with the hurt and pain that day caused all of his life. The more he squeezed his ears and his head, the more the smell of smoke came to his nostrils and anger consumed him just like it did when he was a teenager after he lit the match killing the man who shot his friend down in the fields. As he crouched down with his eyes tightly shut and his head toward the ground, he felt a hand on his shoulder. It was Rain's father, but because Paton had no idea he followed him into the woods, he swung out, fighting like a mad man until Mr. Kennedy shouted his name in such a deep tone that he thought it was his own father. His father was the only man who'd ever raised his voice at him, so when it happened, Paton stood at attention and got his thoughts back together as he stared Mr. Kennedy directly in his eyes.

Although Mr. Kennedy didn't fully understand what was going on with Paton, what he did know was that Paton needed to get back to the house because the baby had been born just as fast as he ran away. Paton wiped his eyes from where they'd been blurred up by tears that he refused to let fall, and Mr. Kennedy held out his arm to let Paton know that everything was fine, then he walked on by his father-in-law like the man that he was supposed to be. When they got back to the house, Mr. Kennedy never said a word about what happened in the woods minutes prior.

"Paton, come on see our new baby girl," Rain smiled after Paton closed the door behind her mom. Rain hadn't stopped smiling since she looked into the eyes of baby girl

Jocelyn, but when Paton held his baby girl the first time in his arms yesterday, he felt an enormous sense of satisfaction that his family was beginning. Jocelyn was the splitting image of Rain, and he was immensely happy that Rain seemed to be feeling much better than she was when she was pregnant.

"Alright, alright, lemme get her from you. You need to do something?"

"Hold her head, Paton, hold on to her now. Don't let her fall. I have to make it to the bathroom, so take care of her now."

"I got my baby girl," he smiled. "I got her...and the last thing I'm gonna do is let her drop from my arms, even if I'm a dead man. She'll be wrapped in my arms, not even touchin' this here ground."

"Well, that's alright, but just sit down on my chair 'cause if you do pass on, least you won't fall," she snickered. "And stop all that talk about dyin'. I need you to be my man for a long time, Mister Paton Jones. Your daughter needs you, too."

She kissed him quickly and then hurried off into the bathroom as Paton watched behind her until she shut the bathroom door. Then, he went back to sit down with baby Jocelyn cradled inside his arms. She was fast asleep without a care in the world, and Paton considered himself her protector with his own life. As he began to admire her, he also began to check her feet and toes, something he hadn't done since she'd been born.

"Hey there, baby girl. I'm your daddy. Paton," he whispered. "Look just like your mama, girl, just like her. Gonna be beautiful just like her, too. Don't look a thing like me yet, but I know it's coming. Ain't no girl child supposed to look like an ole man no how, ain't it? Now," he continued, changing her position in his arms, "Your grandma, who done gone to be with God, now she's the one who I know I'm gonna see in you. She's gonna be right there in your face or hands somewhere as you get older, and I'll have my mama right back. See there…people can't never die. We just keeps on going in our children."

He talked and sang to Jocelyn every single night. There wasn't a night or day that went by without Paton being the father that he wanted to be to his daughter. As a matter of fact, one complete year after Jocelyn was born, Rain ended up pregnant again . The second baby was a boy, and his name was Junior. In that same year, however, came much trouble.

"Where is it, Rain?" Paton questioned her, furiously shoving the mat away from the boarded up hole that was in the floor. "I can't find it, Rain! You got to tell me where it is now. I mean it!"

"Paton, I don't know," she whimpered, holding Junior in her right arm while Jocelyn held on to her leg.

"You the only person who knows where I keep all our money, Rain. Put Junior down and come over here and look. Come over here and look!" he shouted, and immediately, Rain placed Junior down on the floor next to Jocelyn to go see just what Paton was so upset about. He'd never shouted at her ever before, and this is the first time that he'd ever scared her or the children with his anger.

He kneeled down on the floor and pointed into an empty and dusty hole. Paton kept all the money he ever saved in his lifetime in a bag beneath the floor in their bedroom. It was the only monetary security he had for his family, to keep for his children, while he added to it little by little every time he got paid so that it could grow, just like his father taught him to do. That way, even if he lost a job, he could still feed his family and children.

As he looked down into the empty hole in the floor, he stood back up and looked at a fearful Rain who was shaking in tears. "Paton, I don't…"

"Get down there and put your hand in there, Rain. Hurry up!" Paton's nostrils flared up and down as he stared at Rain as if she'd taken the money and done something with it.

"Paton, don't yell at me! The children are right there behind us, and you scarin' everybody," she cried, which caused Paton to calm down immediately when he stared into Rain's teary eyes. Just like it was yesterday, he heard his mother telling him to calm down, and like an obedient child, his demeanor softened. Then, he reached over and embraced Rain with a heartfelt apology.

"I'm sorry, baby." With his two children looking on, he continued as he stared back at Rain hopelessly. "I got nothin'. I got nothin' to care for you with. It's all gone," he stated with no emotion left. At that, he walked beyond his children and out of the house as Rain stood there staring into the empty hole.

While Paton walked away from his home, sadness took over his entire body. He hadn't felt so low in such a long time, and although he had plenty food in the kitchen to last his family about two weeks, if he didn't find that money, he would have to start all over again. To save that much money now that he had a family would take a lifetime.

He was on his way to Janie's house. She was the only one that he could talk to that had money left to her from their deceased folks, but she was running out of it because of her increased drinking. In the last two years, Janie got more and more hooked to the bottle, and the more she drank, the more men came into her bed at night. It was to a point where Paton just stopped coming over, but today was different. She was the only one close that could help him without causing him to feel ashamed.

As he approached the steps of the house, he saw Janie on the side of the house cutting off vines that were growing up towards the roof. Before she noticed him, he'd already made his way to where she was, picking up the bottle of vinegar in the process.

"Oh hey, Pate," she said as she blew smoke from her mouth as she spit out a cigarette. "You come to help me get this stuff off the house. It comes back like it wants to swallow the house whole…"

"You smokin' now?"

"Ain't your business. You see me with something in my mouth?"

"Not anymore."

"Well, I guess I don't smoke anymore either. If you see me again with a cigar in my mouth then I guess I just picked up the habit again for that day." She looked at the vinegar in his hand. "Are you fixin' to pour it or not, Pate?"

Paton held up the bottle of vinegar over the root of the vine and let it flow out. As the vinegar flowed, he visualized his family being eaten from the outside in by some unknown thing, and as the vinegar hit the ground, he lifted the bottle and hurled it at the house, breaking it to pieces.

The vinegar splattered everywhere, including on Janie, and the vine dropped to the ground as she pulled back the shears in her hand, ready to protect herself from her own brother.

Her hands were shaking like a reed in the wind as she watched the veins in Paton's neck disturb his skin so much that it buckled under all the pressure. "Paton, Paton," she repeated an unknown number of times because she'd never known what to say to calm him down. "It's alright, Pate, just calm down," she stated, backing away from him with the shears still in her hand. It was only when she saw him fall to his knees in agony, groaning so loudly that she thought he was in some kind of danger from the inside out. She then threw the shears to the ground and dove right up next to her brother who was before her on the wet grass sobbing like she hadn't heard him sob since they buried their mother.

"What is it? What's the matter? Tell me now, just open up your mouth and tell me," she pleaded with him, tears rolling down her cheeks as a result of her being effected by his pain as she has been all of her life.

"It's all gone, Janie," he struggled. "All of it…it's gone. I got…" he choked up, but Janie hugged him tighter, encouraging him to finish what he was saying. "I got two children now, and I got to feed 'em."

"What you sayin'…what's all gone? I got food in there, I got plenty and can get more from the store…" she replied, pointing at the house.

"No! No! All my money!" He punched the brick wall, and the skin on his fist ripped, causing trickles of blood to flow down between his fingers. "I went to go get some money, Janie," he started again while staring her in her eyes, "and all of it was gone. Like a ghost just came in the house and stole all my money. Ain't no bag there…not a bill left in the floor. Nothing."

Janie fell back onto the grass. She knew how long and hard he saved all that money, mostly in preparation for a family like the one he had, so she knew this was one of those things that would take him from good to worse in no time at all. Hesitantly, she raised a question.

"Did you ask Rain…if she knows what done happened to …"

"She ain't say she did. I asked her. I asked her, I yelled at her, and I ask her again," he wept. "Janie, what I'm gone do? I can't even feed my family the way I was doing now. They used to things that I can't even get 'em now, Janie. I'm used to doing what…"

"And you still will, Paton. We gonna just start over. I say us, not just you. I'ma get a message to our big sister January to see if she can sneak some money up from under her husband nasty nose…"

"You won't do nothin'. January got her own set of problems. She always has."

"Well, I got some money," she stated proudly, standing tall over her broken brother. "I got some money, and you can have half what I got. We'll both take care of us, for the rest of our lives we will. What you don't have, I got. You hear me? I'm your sister, and don't you forget it." She looked around at the house. "Ain't got no family in here with me no way, so even if y'all wanna move over here, you welcome."

Paton reached over and leaned desperately on his sister's leg, and while he sobbed thanking her for her help, Janie pulled another cigarette from her pocket, lit it and started smoking once again. This time, she had no interruption from Paton as her hand trembled each time she removed the cigarette from her lips to exhale. Then, she stared down at her brother and knew that he wasn't gonna be the same for a while. This was just something else that was taken from him that he couldn't get back fast…if at all.

Later on that day, Paton went home with some money he'd gotten from Janie. When he walked in the house, he saw Rain breast feeding Junior while Jocelyn ran behind him, tugging on his pant leg calling him daddy. He didn't give any of them a second glance, and when Rain called his name, her voice fell on deaf ears which caused Rain to gather the children, sit them in a crib together, and then go after him.

"Paton, you didn't hear me calling you?" she questioned her husband as he kneeled down at the empty hole. He didn't look up until she called him once again. "Paton?"

He jerked back like he had no idea he'd passed by them when he walked into the house. When he turned back to face her, an unsettled appearance overtook his face, and he just stared at her as if he didn't even know her. After ten long seconds went by, he rested his unforgiving gaze and spoke as he tucked the money he got from his sister into the floor.

"No, I didn't hear you," he said in a low tone. His anger had already kindled against Rain because on the slow walk back home, he couldn't piece together where all the money went with Rain being home the whole time. "I do need to say something to you though, and…" He stood up and walked toward her, staring into the eyes of the woman he loved so dearly. "I only need to say it one time, Rain. Didn't think I would have to say this at all, but since I do…" he continued as a tear fell from his eye as a result of him trying to remain calm while his heart thirsted for revenge against whoever took his life savings. "Don't never let nobody in our room no more." His eyes remained locked onto hers, and Rain's face, although a nice brown tone, nearly lost every bit of color it had.

She began to stutter, "I never let…"

Paton then leaned in closer to her face, next to her ear, which caused her to quiet down. "All I'm telling you, Rain, is not to lose sight of our money again…ever. Don't say nothing else. I'm about to go out here and play with my kids." He walked by her as if she was a liar and the truth was far from her, but he couldn't shed the fact that he loved her so much. When he married her, he knew in his heart of hearts that it was his chance to cast away bad times and look forward to good. He wasn't sure about that anymore, and it was Paton's first night not sleeping.

All night long, he looked at a sleeping Rain lying in the bed next to him while his children slept in the other room, and he wondered who the woman was that he married as tears flowed down his face. He wanted to believe her when she said she never let anyone in the room, but he couldn't get himself to do it fully. There was always something in the back of his head that was unsure about her, but the one thing that Paton was sure about was that Rain had no idea that all his stolen money was marked. He never told her.

When Paton was a boy, his father would hide money as well. That was where Paton learned the habit. Only one person was supposed to know where it was, so if it came up missing, his father would say that was the one to blame. The other thing about the money that John Lee Jones told Paton before he left the face of the earth was that all the money was marked. Every single to every ten and on upward. He'd mark the money by laying one bill on top of the other each time he got extra, and he would only let the two corners of the bills show from underneath the top bill. After that, he would take a fountain pen and run it down the line of bills so that he mark would hit the same spot on the front of the bill – the bottom right. When Paton got his share of the money, after his father died, he laid the bills the opposite way his father laid them, and marked through them with the same kind of pen. His mark ran straight through his father's line, crossing it like an upside down letter T. That was Paton's mark for his money, the money that he knew one day, he would see again, thus finding the man or woman who took it.

For the next five years, Paton's outlook on life took a turn for the worse, in the midst of Rain's father passing away of a sudden heart attack during the first half of those years. Although he tried to hide it, the anger behind someone coming into his home and snatching what belonged to him and his family only built each time he put more money down inside the hole. Rain wanted to go to work, but he wouldn't let her leave until the children grew old enough to at least clean themselves off and take good direction from others. On top of that, he wanted her to be at home for the full day, so that if his money went missing again from the same spot, he would know she had everything to do with it. Nothing ever came up missing again.

Paton became extremely paranoid, although he was the best father to his children, despite the fact that with every year, he became disturbed by his daughter Jocelyn. As she grew up, she and Junior looked vastly different. He noticed that Junior looked just like him and Rain, however, with Jocelyn, he saw no parts of him nor his family's side of the family inside her. Jocelyn was all parts of Rain from the head to the toe, and besides that, she had her very own look all to herself. When she was first born, Paton thought nothing of her looks because children change, but as time went by, her looks never came closer to his as Junior's did.

Despite, his thoughts about Jocelyn, he also tried to continue in the role he played as Rain's loving husband, but sometimes when he looked at her, he held so much resentment behind a feeling he just couldn't put his finger on. If he could put his finger on it, he would kill it, so that he could move on with his life. Unfortunately, there he was in love with a woman that he was becoming unsure of with every day that passed as he thought about how his money came up missing. Even when she read the Bible, he wanted to go back behind her and flip through the pages to be certain she wasn't keeping something from him inside the pages that were supposed to be nothing but truth. He never thought he'd gotten the complete truth from Rain, so every day, just to make her feel comfortable, he would behave normally. However, it was all orchestrated, and this same orchestration became how he lived day to day just to get by. Every movement and emotion was by design, except for his anger which fought its way out in his dreams. The only person he continued to rely on was his sister Janie.

"You been able to save some money, ain't you? Here some more to help out," she offered, her hand out with a fist full of dollar bills.

"How you gettin' this extra money so easy, Janie?"

"The folks I work for pays me good for my service."

"You ain't never told me who you work for since you got another gig. Maybe I can do something for 'em, too, being that they cut me back."

Janie cut her eyes over at him, and then put her eyes back on the road ahead, ignoring the question. "Ain't nothing for you to do, 'cept if you wanna do woman's work, and ain't no brother of mine gonna do woman's work."

"And what you call woman's work there, Janie?" he laughed. "I can sew. Give me a piece of thread and a needle, I can make a hem just as good as the rest of y'all," he laughed. "Say it ain't so?"

"I bet you can, Pate, but…the people I work for only hire women," she stated with her head hanging low, but her chest still high and proud. "They take me out of town and then bring me back here. That's all I require of 'em, so I can live without people knowing." Paton snatched her by her arm, and she fought her way loose. "You need money, ain't it! Just how you think I been getting it? Ain't a job in this town pay me like this, and I only got to work two days out the week. I just take my clothes off, and then I put 'em back on. I ain't no whore though! That I ain't! They look at me, I move around and then I leave. I get my cut. Out of my cut, you get yours. Lots of ladies do it, 'specially ones that's like me."

"And what's wrong with you, Janie? Huh? What!" Paton yelled, saddened by the news of his sister turning into a nude dancer.

"I ain't got no man to keep me in a house and love me! Either I live and make the money I can, or I live and die just broke and never loved a day in my whole life. If I can get money…well, at least I can get that. If some folks woulda' stole my money, where would that have left me? I got nobody, and if you dead, I really am by myself and have to move in with our sister who stuck herself. 'Sides, my body they can't get enough of," she smirked, but Paton didn't flinch a muscle. After watching her brother turn his head away from her, Janie gave him a nudge to which he didn't respond. Instead of responding verbally, he reached down in his pocket and gave her the money back that she'd given him.

"I don't need your money no more. I'm going back home. I'll work round the clock before I take anymore money from you."

"That ain't nothin'!" she refused him giving the money back. "I'm gonna still do it whether you broke or not. That's what I know. Learned it good, and I'm gonna keep going, so don't act like it's all about you that I'm…"

Paton reached around, grabbed her by her throat, and lifted her off the ground. "I said I ain't taking your money no more. None of it!" Then, he dropped her straight to the ground and walked the rest of the way to the store alone.

"And this how you gonna do me? Out here in the open…front of all these people, Pate! I'm your sister, and I'm always gonna be…for life…no matter what I do," she screamed, punching the ground with her fists while a woman ran out to the road to get her, but Janie pushed away from her in disgust, especially when she laid eyes on the woman's husband. It made Janie feel worthless, but she stood back to her feet anyway, stuck her chest out and walked back to her home while puffing on a cigarette. As soon as she got home, she opened a drink and swallowed it down, pushing her sorrows down deeper than ever before.

Back where she was abandoned, Paton had already made his way up the road to the store. He still had a couple of dollars in his pocket, and that could get him some bread, meat and other things that the family needed while he was out looking for more work. As he entered, the clerk recognized him and nodded, and Paton reciprocated while his thoughts became more jumbled than they'd been in a long time. He walked to the shelf, got some of the items that he thought he needed for the home, and then slowly got in the line.

Paton had grown anxious over the years when he went into a crowd of more than two since he was robbed of his money. Things went from straight to crooked in his life, and he trusted no one. As he got in the short line, there was a woman paying at the counter, and after her was a man slightly shorter than he was, and Paton was third. Thoughts of how he would pay his sister back for all she'd done compounded the stress that he'd already been under for years. Even when he got up in the morning to look himself in the mirror, he saw a different man, a strained man who was still in his early life but felt like he was sixty instead of in his thirties.

The line moved and so did he, and he watched as the man pulled out his wallet. It was a habit that had already become intrusive to his daily living – staring at money on a mission to find his own. Paton watched as the man did something he never did and that was show all his bills in one place. He learned from his father to never show his whole hand to anyone, so as he watched the man thumb through dollar bills like he was showing off, he took a closer look at the two dollar bills that he pulled out of his wallet. There were the marks, the marks that he hadn't seen in years, they were finally right there before his eyes.

Paton's breathing rose to a pace that he'd only known at one other time in his life, when he wanted to kill Drowning Boy's killer. Taken in the disbelief that a man stood in front of him with his marked money, he continued to examine what he felt was his opportunity for the ultimate justice. The bread that was held inside his hand started to shrink from the pressure being placed on it from the grinding of his fingers into his palm as he formed a tight fist. He watched as the clerk took the money from the man's hand and gave him change back. At that particular point, Paton had only memorized the back of the man's head, but as he turned around with a brown bag of food in his arm, his face became a reality. It was the most amazing thing to Paton as the man slowly walked by him. Paton felt extremely familiar with the stranger, but before he could reach out and grab the man's shoulder, the unknown man glanced up to say a friendly hello to the rest of the people in line, then coincidentally, met the eyes of Paton. In what could be described as a scripted reaction of guilt, the unidentified man shuddered in a chilling pause when his light brown eyes met the bold and threatening eyes of the man whose whole life had been a series of devastating losses from the time he was a teenager. After coming face to face with Paton, he took three more steps toward the exit in an attempt to mask his guilt while Paton appeared stunned in place by his every move, examining any signs of guilt made by the man who wore the cleanest pair of navy blue shoes and dark slacks he'd seen in a while.

Only a second more went by before the items that Paton had in his hands were released to meet the dusty floor right beside his work boots, and when the impact of the groceries hitting the ground was heard, the man with the marked money, dropped his bag of food and took off running. Paton, then, chased him like a wild man, shoving anyone in his way out of the path that led him to the man he now knew stole his life savings. It wasn't long before Paton caught up to him as the man's slick shoes had him sliding all over the ground in his failing efforts to get away. In one dive, Paton grabbed the back of his shirt and threw him to the ground with so much force, blood oozed from his head after it bounced off of the rocky ground. It took no time for Paton to straddle him like a wolf on a defenseless sheep. With his hand squeezing the life from the neck of his prey, Paton's fist repeatedly beat the left side of his face until blood leaked from his nose and mouth. After a continuous amount of blows, Paton lifted the man's head from the ground by his collar expecting an answer to the question he felt he didn't have to ask verbally – where was the rest of his money? Instead of the man delivering the answer to Paton's demands that were laid out by fists against his face, he viciously smiled through all the blood that crept out of every crack in his skin. Then, the man's lips began to utter something furthest from Paton's thoughts.

"I done slept with her for years now, even 'fore you married her, Paton," he bragged as he spit thick, red blood from his mouth. "I know 'bout somethin' you don't know 'bout see," he continued as he glanced quickly at people walking toward them, coming from the store. "And that's how I get what I can get from your pretty little wife," he stressed in an evil tone, so evil that Paton raised his arm to hit him again, but stalled at the man's next words. "Because I know about the killin' her and her mama did long time ago. Tried to hide it, but I know 'cause I watched 'em in the woods back then, and I'm the only one sides them who do know. They blew that man's head clean off, and took it underneath they house. I been told her what I saw when she was a girl, and when I want it, I go get it right from in between her legs. See here, you ain't know who you married. All the secrets she been hidin' from you." He pushed his head closer to Paton's face and repeated, "I been going to get my fill of little Mrs. Rain, and if she don't give it to me, I'll tell them police. She knows it. Her and her mama know 'bout that man they killed." he laughed, gaining a thrill from Paton's ignorance, wanting nothing more than to create hatred and hopelessness to the man who just attacked him.

Paton's grip on the man's collar lessened, and he began to wipe the massive amount of blood that he beat from the man's face. The smile was something that he'd seen before, the way his lips curved when he grinned about the terrible news he'd given Paton about his own wife. The man noticed Paton searching his face for something in particular, so he interrupted the stare. "Guess what else I done done to your precious wife, Paton?" he stressed. "Look at me close. I see you already doing it. That little girl don't look nothin' like you, do she? You see it now, don't you, boy? You been taking care of my seed, without me even askin'." Then, he scooted slowly from underneath a now stunned and weakened Paton who rested on his knees, his throat quaking from what he saw as true with his very own eyes. "These cuts on my face you made ain't nothing. But I tell you what, if you stop takin' care of my baby girl… me and Rain's baby girl… I'll take your wife from you just as easy as I took your money from under your nose. She was scared to tell you 'cause she happen to love you like the air she breathe, so she had to sleep with me and gimme all that money 'less I take her life without even touchin' her…take her family and her freedom," he smiled, repaying Paton back in words what Paton gave him in fists while enjoying every moment.

Paton didn't know what to say or do. His body was frozen as he stared back at the man whom he still didn't know by name. The man had already slid all the way from underneath Paton at that point, but he didn't rush to get up from the ground. He relished in breaking Paton down to nothing on the inside. "My baby girl looks good there, Paton, huh? She look just like me, ain't it? Thank you…and for your wife." He paused to continue wiping the blood from his dirty face, and that was when Paton finally spoke.

"Come near my wife again, and I'll kill you dead. I'll kill you over and over again 'til ain't nothing left to kill…"

"Like you kill that man way back then, Paton?" he confidently retorted as he squinted his bloodshot and puffy eye while tilting his head curiously. "Know what I'm talking 'bout, ain'tcha? Ole reliable, drunk Jesse there like to talk to people he think are his friends when he been on that bottle. Ain't that right? Settin' roofs on fire with white men inside won't sit too well with them lynchin' white boys out there, will it now?" he threatened Paton, and at those words, Paton lunged at him, ready to kill him. The next words from the man's mouth was the only thing that stopped him.

"It's alright, everybody! This here Paton Jones. Y'all know him, ain't it? Got himself a temper on him, but I forgive him. Thought he knew me from somewhere, somehow…thought I was the one who been takin'…" He stared back into Paton's eyes and revealed more secret details about his family. "His sister outta town. Ain't me though. Ain't me."

Immediately, Paton turned away from his trance, looked over his shoulder and saw a pack of people, some even holding their grocery bags, horrified at the bloody scene that was before their eyes. One of the onlookers called out, "Haslem, you alright? Need to get that looked at mighty fast because he put a whoopin' on you something awful there, man."

Another onlooker called out for Paton, even came and grabbed him up from the ground. "Paton, man, hey… you done 'bout beat that man to death. Who he? What he do, man? He done stole somethin' from you or what?" At that question, Paton stiffened up and refused to speak, afraid of what else the man he just beat up might say to the crowd. What the man whom he now knew as Haslem took from him, he couldn't beat away or kill away, and it was no sense in letting anybody know because whatever got out, would cost him his life. "Paton? Paton?" the man continued, until he understood by Paton's stance that he wasn't going to answer. Therefore, he shrugged his shoulders and waved the crowd off. "Just trying to help you out, Pate."

Paton never even looked back at the dispersing crowd again. Instead, he only watched as a bloody Haslem walked away. Paton didn't move until he could no longer see him, and while he stood there, he'd never felt as trapped inside his own skin as he did then. When Haslem turned the corner, making himself fall out of sight, it was only then that Paton started to walk forward emotionlessly toward the only place he could go. The only place he felt safe…back to Janie's house.

As he walked, his stomach felt sick and his nerves shattered as his mind replayed over and over again the day before he found the money missing and how Rain was having sexual relations with that same man over and over again for years. He thought about them in his bed and how when he got home, the sheets were still hanging out to dry while she'd already put another sheet on the mattress. A tear came down Paton's eye as he watched Rain, in his mind, smile at him as soon as he came through the door that day. She smelled the same and looked exactly the same as when he left her that morning…beautiful.

Passing by the turn that would have taken him back home, he continued to walk beyond it, not even looking that way as he thought about the only family he had left in the whole entire world that he could call his very own. Each time his mind wandered off to Jocelyn, he cringed, choking back the tears that he'd been tricked into believing that Jocelyn was his child, even by Rain. He allowed his thoughts to tarry back to the day she was throwing up and crying about being pregnant. She was scared to death for no real reason, but now Paton knew why. He knew everything, and it caused him to start running as fast as he could toward Janie's house.

When he got there, she wasn't home, and the first thing he went in search of was the item that Janie offered him to drown out his heartaches and thoughts of the past and present – a bottle of alcohol. His heart was hurting so badly that all he wanted to do was leave the earth and pretend his life had never been. Although everything he heard about his family was brand new, his mind kidnapped him and took him all the way back to the moment Drowning Boy died.

When Paton burst into Janie's bedroom, he found on top of her dresser and bed half empty bottles and ones that were completely full. He snatched the first jug he saw, and without even knowing what it was, he drank. With each swallow followed another one right behind it until he choked, but he continued to drink. The rage he had for Haslem drove him to drink even more, and his thoughts of wanting to strangle him to death grew more vivid than they were when he was right in front of him.

Paton took an empty bottle and threw it against the wall, causing it to break into pieces. Then, as he dropped against the wall and slid to the floor, he reached out and grabbed two more bottles and drank them down. Altogether, he drank six straight down, the pain from his heartache took over his entire being, causing him to destroy whatever was in his sight. As he pulled down photos and destroyed walls with his bare hands, he could barely stand up, so he fell up against the door frame as he made his way toward the living room where he lifted the couch and threw it up against the wall, knocking a plant over with it that Janie had been growing for years. The soil from the potted plant went everywhere and he fell down into the dirt, his knees hitting the floor first and then his face in the palms of his hand.

Moans of agony echoed off the walls of the somewhat empty living room, and all Paton could see was Haslem hanging him up by his neck with a rope and him laughing as the two white men he burned up in that house tugged hard on the noose with huge smiles on their faces while Drowning

Boy stood in front of him lying in a pool of blood. Paton then fell completely onto his stomach, grabbing his head as he was in excruciating pain, and when he looked up, he saw his wife and son while off to the side was Jocelyn. She was staring at him solemnly and then she started to smile…with the identical smile as her birth father.

"Come to me, baby," a voice called from his left side. It was his mother's voice, and immediately he turned his attention to the far corner of the room where he saw his mom standing there calling for him.

"Mama," he cried with a wail so profound that if the dead could walk, they would. He watched her beckon him over to her with her hand, but as he began to crawl toward her presence, she dissolved while calling his name. "Mama!" he yelled, sobbing tremendously as he fell back onto his side with his arm outstretched to her as she faded away. "I can't do this no more, Mama, please!"

"Do what, boy?" a powerful voice came from the opposite side of the room while the daughter he thought was his continued to smile as blood covered her face, and it began to conform more to the face of her real father.

"Get away from me!" he shoved himself backwards until his back rammed into the table. "Move back before I kill you!"

"Paton! Get up!" the voice ordered, and he stared beyond the wall of the house until an image crept out of it that was shaped like his father.

"But, pops, if you would just listen to me for once. I couldn't handle that, daddy, please! I just need your help…"

"Get up, Paton!" Suddenly, the image charged him, and a drunken Paton sat up to attention the best he could.

When he spoke again to his father, however, his voice turned into that of a boy.

"Daddy, please listen to me," he pleaded with his hands reached out to him. "That boy…he hit me too hard. I just couldn't get up fast enough. I didn't try to let him beat me, but I couldn't see…I just needed you to help me…" Paton continued, recalling a horrible childhood incident when he was only eight years old, but then paused as he stood up to face his father man to man. "I just needed you to help me get up! I needed you to stop him from pounding on my face, daddy! And I am a man!" he yelled ferociously, saliva streaming from his mouth while the tears dried up in the presence his father. "You ain't help me!"

His father turned his back and walked away as Paton tried to grab him and turn him back around so he would listen. With each step John Lee Jones took, the worse Paton felt. "You ain't never listen to me! I ain't as strong as you, pops. Stop walkin' away! And yep, I bet I proved it to you, didn't I? I killed both them men. Both of 'em. I did better than fightin' back, now how 'bout that, pops! Talk to me!" He turned to the area where his mother was standing, stumbled over toward it and curled into a ball on the floor. "Mama! Mama, please…I can't…I can't pray no more," he wept. "I can't…"

The night ended with Paton on the floor, shuddering while surrounded by ghosts and hallucinations of his past and present that not even sleeping could make disappear. For the whole night, Janie never came back home, and Paton fell in and out of nightmares until the sun came back up in the sky. However, the nightmare, this particular time, never left. When he opened his eyes the next morning, he was hunched over on the floor with is head peering out over his knees with Janie hovering over him with a cold rag and ice water while tears ran down her face.

"Paton, get up now. Get up," she said anxiously while nervously continuing to glance around the house at the mess he made in the house. "Paton, it's me. I'm home now. Get on up so you can…"

When she started talking, Paton suddenly reached up and grabbed her by both her arms, causing her to drop the cold rag she prepared for him. Janie stood there in horror because she didn't know what her brother was going to do next or all of what he'd already done. Paton's fingers pressed into her skin until the force behind his touch started to hurt her bones.

"Paton, stop. Cut it out. It hurts…you hurtin' me," she explained, pulling away from him as hard as she could, but it didn't work. He overpowered her rather easily as she continued to fight and kick, only to end up falling to the ground in fear. Paton then hovered over her, causing her to feel smaller than a rat in the tall grass. "Paton, it's me! It's Janie! Wake up!" she screamed, scared of becoming the victim of a horrible beating. There was only one time Paton got hold to her in her life after he started having nightmares, and it was six months after Drowning Boy was killed. It was at that time that Paton walked into her room in the middle of the night and started punching her over and over again. If it wasn't for their mom Sarah jumping up from her sleep after hearing her screams to come and grab Paton off of her, Janie would have ended up under the mercy of his fists for longer than two minutes.

As Paton stood there hanging his head low over Janie, he looked at her with a confused gaze, the same gaze that she was accustomed to, and then he stepped over her to walk away. He didn't say one thing to her, and all the mess he made went untouched as he opened the front door and left. Janie, still shaken, picked herself up from the floor and ran back to her room to cry. When she got there, she fell up against the door when she noticed that every single liquor bottle was either broken or gone. That was when she knew something had gone terribly wrong with her only brother because he never drank one ounce of liquor.

Immediately, she thought that she'd drove him to drink based off of what she'd told him earlier about dancing for men. She gave the place one more look over, and noticed the huge holes in the walls and the way he junked the room over. Then, she got the nerve to run behind him, so she bolted down the hallway and out the door where she found Paton sitting on the bottom step staring out at much of nothing.

"Paton, you drank all my drink in there? You did that?" she asked nervously, holding on tightly to the door knob. "You feel alright…because you ain't no drinker? Something the matter with…"

Paton stood up slowly, and then he turned around like he was being held onto by something that didn't want to release him. There was nothing smooth about the way he moved his feet or his body, but when he finally turned to face her, there was nothing different about his face at all. He didn't look to have been weeping, and there was no anger at all. Nothing was there. Then, he opened his mouth.

"Ain't nothing wrong, Janie. I just had a late night is all, and I been having them nightmares again. So I drank all of it 'till I fell asleep."

She glanced back into her house, and then back at Paton. "You don't remember nothing from last night?" she asked. With all the mess he made, she was sure something was wrong but he wasn't revealing what it was.

"Should I?" he asked.

"No…nothing. I'm 'bout to go to bed. You head on home, Paton," Janie stated, clearly not wanting him to come back in the house.

Paton smiled at his sister's remark. His teeth were whiter than the morning clouds overhead. Then, before she could even ask him about his questionable grin which made her feel odd on her own porch, he turned back around and made his way off the land. His gait was strong and powerful, like a man who was just promoted on his job. As Janie watched him walk away, she just attributed his actions toward the amount of alcohol he guzzled down overnight. She took a deep breath, calmed down, and then smiled.

"He drunk," she laughed, shaking her head, relieved that he'd found a way to make it through the night since he'd confessed that those living nightmares had come back to haunt him. On the way back inside the dump Paton created, Janie didn't feel as bad or nervous as she felt at first. "It'll take time for him to be able to hold his liquor." She laughed one more time, pulled out the money she made from her bra, and then sat down to grab a half bottle of wine Paton missed. "At least he didn't take my good stuff." She drank her last bottle after having been awake all night…dancing for strange men.

As Paton walked down the road, a few cars passed by him with drivers who recognized him, even offering him a ride. To their surprise, Paton continued to stare forward, not giving them a second look. He was on his way to the field where old Drowning Boy was killed. Really, he was on the way to the house that used to stand on that same land before it burned to the ground. He felt like he needed to go there, so that was where his feet carried him.

On the way and a little beyond the store where he first laid eyes on Haslem, the owner of the store was just opening up to set up his shop when he glanced over and saw Paton in the same clothes as he wore the day of the scuffle. As the owner swept up around the small building, he yelled over at Paton and asked how he was getting along. When he didn't get an answer from him, he put his broom down and walked over to him. Paton continued to walk.

"Slow down, Paton. I hear 'bout what went on after you chased that fellow Haslem out the store there. What was that there all about? I know you, son, and you ain't not never chased a man out my store like I seen you do that day."

Paton's eyes never even turned his way. Instead of answering with words, he answered with the same grin he gave Janie back on the porch and kept walking. The store owner thought that to be odd because of how he and Paton always socialized quite a bit at the store. They were good friends in his eyes, so he was baffled when all he got from Paton was a grin.

"Paton, you doin' alright?" he asked as he took the back of his hand and slapped him over the arm. Before his arm even left the side of Paton's shirt, Paton's right hand grabbed him by his collar and shoved him, nearly knocking him to the ground.

"Hey! Keep your hands off me, man. You got problems there, Paton...serious ones, too!" he shouted at a glaring Paton, but he dared not retaliate. The man he knew as Paton wasn't the same, and he knew it by the way Paton stared back at him, like he didn't know him from the dirt beneath his feet even though they'd lived in the same spot since forever. The store owner contained himself as he stood strong back on the side of Paton but immediately felt for his old friend. "If something's going on, man, just say something. It's me, man, Redd. Mr. Redd. Wake up, man." Just then, he smelled the odor of alcohol as Paton let breath come forth from his nostrils. A confused appearance draped across his face as he backed away from Paton, and Paton continued his walk toward the creek.

As Paton neared the creek, his eyes bolted to the path he took on the way to the house he burned down. While walking, he began hallucinating again, seeing Drowning Boy standing behind various trees as he passed by. The only time he shuddered was when their eyes would meet, but when Paton got too close to Drowning Boy's image, he would disappear and end up ten trees in front of him. By the time Paton reached the empty lot where the house once stood, Drowning Boy was standing there directly in the center of it. Blood began to pour from his wounds and as the emotions of that day returned to Paton, the white man that shot him suddenly appeared. He had a gun in his hand. He raised it high and then lowered it to the side of Drowning Boy's head, pulled the trigger and shot him dead again. As Drowning Boy's body fell to the ground, Paton rushed toward the man who shot him, something that he felt he should have done a long time ago. As he reached the man with the gun, a smile crept across the white man's face in the shape of Haslem's, causing Paton to strip the gun from his hand and shoot him in his face. Hate filled every part of Paton's heart, and before he put the gun down, Jocelyn, the daughter he thought was his, appeared beneath him. She was playing in the dirt at the head of Drowning Boy's body. As she played, he watched her as if she was the enemy, and the more he watched, the faster she played until her playing became so rapid that she stopped. In an instant, she twisted her head back, her eyes staring back into whom she knew as her father's eyes, and then she smiled…Haslem's smile. Paton rose his gun and shot her. He unloaded the gun, but she wouldn't die. She just continued to laugh at him continuously, and John Lee's voice came into his ear.

"Don't let nobody break you, boy. Nobody!" His father's voice felt like a calm wind to his ears while his mother's voice was only a loud whisper that he couldn't hear although she shouted while standing right in front of him. Her eyes were blood shot and her veins popped out from both sides of her neck as she strained to get her words out, but Paton couldn't hear her. The only voice he heard was his father's, and it was louder than thunder, but one that gave him direction that matched his emotions on the inside. That was the way he went, and for the first time in his life, he stopped fighting to hear his mother. Suddenly, she disappeared along with everyone else, including the gun that was inside his hand, and he finally stood on the land all alone.

"Paton!" Rain ran out of the house like she'd been apart from him for a lifetime. There had never been a time when he didn't come home, so for him to have stayed out all night long was a lifetime to her. Junior was in the house crying because he was hungry for what he wanted to eat and not what was on his plate while Jocelyn was playing with a little doll on the floor in front of the front door. Paton could see her from the short distance he was away from the house until Rain stopped in front of him. "Paton, you didn't come home last night," she stated, wiping her hands off on an apron. "Did you find another job, is that why you didn't come back?" As she finished speaking, it didn't take her long to smell the stench of alcohol coming from his pores. "You been drinkin'? Huh?" she sniffed. "You been drinkin', Paton?"

He touched her arm and pulled her out of the way by her elbow. His concentration was on Jocelyn first and then her. As he stared at Jocelyn, she didn't look back up at him. Instead, she continued to play with her doll. Then, he turned back to his wife who was busy inspecting him as if she knew he was hiding something.

"I ain't been doing much of nothing. Had me some drinks." He then took a roller from her head with his right hand, allowing her hair to fall into her face. "What you been doing…while I been gone?" He then nodded toward Jocelyn. "You and Jocie…what y'all been doin'?"

Rain backed away, confused at the jovial way Paton sounded while playing with her hair after he'd been gone overnight. She removed her elbow from his hand and grew uneasy as Paton moved his eyes back and forth between herself and Jocelyn, then she quickly replied to make the staring stop.

"Nothing…we were…I was waiting on you to get back home," she stammered, snatching the roller back from his hand to place it back in her hair "You staring at me like I'm the one was gone away from home."

"You wasn't, were you? You been here the whole time." He called her back over to him with his finger, and she went to him nervously. This was a Paton she wasn't familiar with. He was talking in riddles. The Paton she knew was always up front and to the point. This one she had to figure out.

"Where else I'm gonna go with two children?" she asked as he leaned in and kissed her on her forehead while again, looking at Jocelyn who had finally looked up to see him. Paton quickly turned his focus onto Rain.

"That's a good question. Let me go see about my children…both of my children." Then, he kissed her on her lips with breath that reeked from the foulness of an night and day with no hygiene upkeep. Rain smelled it all, but she didn't complain nor did she pull back. There was a pit in the deepest parts of her intestines that made her feel sick because if her senses were telling her the truth about Paton, it was that he found out something about a man that she'd long gotten rid of...or so she thought. Despite all her thoughts, she kept quiet.

Not willing to walk back into the house with him until she calmed down and got her thoughts together, she watched him as he cleared the steps to enter the house. He stood over Jocelyn who then stood up, holding her doll up to him like she wanted him to see her favorite doll. She'd been pretending to feed it food and wash it with a small bowl of water that her mom placed on the floor for her to make believe. Paton would normally pick her up and give her a huge kiss on the cheek, and right after that, he'd tickle her until she couldn't laugh anymore. Rain stood back and noticed that today was the only day that he didn't greet her in that manner, and she was reluctant to blame it on the alcohol. She was more concerned with what drove him to it, but she couldn't question him because she believed that he would then begin questioning her.

That night, when Rain tucked the children in their beds and came to join Paton in their bedroom, she became aware of the way he looked at her when she prepared to join him underneath the sheets. She was accustomed to Paton undressing her, and even bathing her in water he'd drawn with his own hands, but that night was different. Paton's behavior was purely driven on his own pleasure, and he wanted her to comfort him.

"Take your clothes off, Rain." Paton was lying on the bed completely naked, half of his body underneath the clean sheets. Rain laughed at first because she wasn't aware that he wanted her to truly follow through, but then, he leaned forward slightly, met her eyes, and repeated, "Take your clothes off, and when you're done, I want you to stand there for me."

"Paton, why you want me to stand up in front of you...naked? Why you acting so..." she started but stopped when he lifted his hand.

"Ain't I your husband? You beautiful, Rain, and I want to see you. Can't a man look at his wife...or would you feel better if I was another man?" He leaned even closer and watched the skin on her body stiffen. It brought him satisfaction to watch her continue in her life of lies, so he was willing to take it as far as she was willing to go.

As soon as those words came from Paton's lips, Rain's night gown fell to the floor, and then Paton asked her to turn all the way around so that he could admire her. In Paton's mind, he was certain that a man like Haslem had gotten more from his wife than he'd ever asked for. A jealousy raged inside him that only death could cure, but he wanted more from the lies and deceit that stole from him. He wanted his life with his wife back, but he knew he could never have it again...ever.

As he pulled Rain's naked body closer to him with his outstretched hand, she crawled on top of the bed and then on top of his warm, naked body. She kissed him, and he kissed her back. That was the last kiss he'd given her before he stopped making love to her with his entire being. As he watched her on top of him and her beneath him, she became like any other woman because all his emotion was wiped away. Rain even felt it. Everything became one big act...until he found something else to play with.

"May," Rain cried as she sat beside her older sister in the bedroom of their parents home. May was there temporarily because their mother Sunflower caught something close to the flu. The doctor said it could be more than a week before she got better, so until then, May would be the woman of the house and take care of everything until she got well.

May was great with pulling whatever weight she had to pull. She'd been doing it all of her life, and this time was no different. Before their deceased father was able to make more money, it was May who had to drop from school to help with everything around the house. It was over fifteen years later that Rain was born, so May was just like a mom to her just as much as she was a sister.

"What's wrong wit'chu, Rain? You look like you about to cry a cloud full of tears, and you ain't got a reason to in the world," she rambled, almost as if she didn't want Rain to get another word in edgewise. "You got a good family, and even though you fell on hard times, you been taught how to make it on scraps like everybody else round here and them scraps make things look just like normal. Mama done had to put back some since she can't work no more than a certain number of hours…"

"May, this ain't about money!" she yelled as the tears streamed down her face. "Money ain't it. I know how to get a pig and cut it just like the rest of y'all, but it's more than that, May. I need you to listen to me, and stop avoidin' like I know you're doing."

May stood up from the bed and walked out of the bedroom. That was Rain's cue to follow. It was something they did when they were younger. May would have a boy walk by the house, and when she would walk out of the back door, Rain would have a fit about something to make her parents pay attention to her and not May. Rain may have been much younger, but she learned quickly how to beat the watchful eyes of her parents. That was when they were younger though. This time, Rain was following her sister out of the room for a whole other reason, and their mom's sick eyes didn't have enough energy to ease drop.

May walked away from the back step, moving toward the tree that sat in the center of the yard. Rain rushed over to her, and before May even sat down on the straw, Rain started to unload.

"May, Paton's not actin' right. He don't even make love to me the same as he used to do. I feel like I'm a piece of meat more than his wife, and when he does it, he don't even look at me…"

"Beauty fades, baby. I ain't married, but I ain't never heard of no man loving they wife the same after a year of being married to her no how. They start seein' you different while we see them the same. It ain't no nother woman is it, baby sister?"

"Another woman?" Rain asked in disbelief. "Ain't no woman in they right mind want no drunk! He came to the house after drinkin' all night. May, he was so stank and starin' at me like he don't even know me. Since then, ain't nothing been the same. It's been weeks, May, weeks! I feel like I don't even know him, like he ain't part of me no more."

May said nothing for a couple of seconds, and then she stood up from the ground to lean her body on the tree. Rain looked up at her, waiting for an answer to her problems, but the answer she got was one she didn't want to hear.

"You ain't heard 'bout Paton lately?"

"What you mean?" Rain stood up and stared confused into her sister's face.

"You know I don't take nothing to do with no gossip, but I hear from a friend of mine that your husband been fightin'. What was that fight about? He didn't tell you, Rain?"

"I ain't hear 'bout no fight. Ain't nobody come tell me…why ain't nobody tell me?" she questioned her sister highly annoyed with everything that was going on.

May turned back to face her younger sister, and when their eyes met, it was May's eyes that looked like they'd seen a ghost. "Ain't nobody tell you because you ain't left the house until today, is that right?" Rain nodded her head, and May continued. "Seem like Paton going through some things, real bad things, because he near beat a man 'til all the blood ran out his face." It was then that May's next words burned a hole through Rain's body. "They say he beat that man like he'd done something unforgivable. Say the man's name was Haslem."

Rain dropped to the ground like the next place she wanted to go was underneath it to be buried with the dead. All of her strength left her body, but she became sorely afraid to look back into the eyes of her sister. Without anymore hesitation, she then asked, "Did the man…the man named Haslem…did he die?"

"No, that wasn't the word. Word came back to me that he got up and walked way. Paton just stayed there for some time 'til he finally left. Don't nobody know why Paton snapped like he did, but from what people say, it seemed like he was in a rage for only some minutes, then he calmed down. Like he was two different people in one. They say he blacked out." May got as quiet as a mouse and waited on

Rain's response. "You know 'bout this man named Haslem?"

"No," Rain said immediately, shuffling her dress together, and standing to her feet. "I don't know nobody by that name, May," she denied.

"Don't you lie, girl!" May finally retorted, snatching Rain's hand from her skirt and holding it as tightly as she could. "If you know that man, you tell it," she stressed, "because can't nobody save you back there in them woods from Paton if you done something…"

"I said I ain't know no man named Haslem!" she screamed, snatching her hand away from her sister.

"The Bible say in Proverbs six verses thirty-four and thirty-five that a man can get so jealous if another man been with his wife that he liable to do just about anything in the day of vengeance. He won't rest! I know things 'bout you, Rain…"

"You don't know nothin' about me, May! Nothing!" she cried, covering her ears from whatever she thought May would say next.

"I know you would sneak off sometimes before you married Paton. Where you would be going, I don't know, but I know you would come back real quiet. I remember when I stayed over Thanksgiving time. Nobody seemed to notice, but I did. Remember when I walked in the room behind you? You smelled musty…"

"That's enough!"

"No it ain't!" May shouted as she grabbed her younger sister by the arms and shook her until Rain stopped fighting to put her hands back over her ears. "You tell me the truth because I been in this world much longer than you, and I'ma tell you, if that man and you been seeing one another, either you gonna tell it or you better hide the truth 'til you die. Paton done took good care of you, and he loves you more than any love I done seen from a man to a woman. More than any! What else can mess a man up but another woman or a strange man with his woman? Ain't much else, now is it? Is it?" she shouted.

"No!" Rain cried so loud that May quickly grabbed her mouth and peered back at the house, hoping that her mother didn't hear the cry of anguish that Rain just released.

"Go back home and make sweet. I don't want to know your answer to none of it because I don't want no parts of it. All I know is that you keep being a good wife and help him the best you can. From what the Bible say, a good wife will win in the end, so you win him back to a man that can get good rest at night when he sleep next to you. Ease his mind if you can. Whatever bothering him, it'll fall off in time."

Rain continued to cry, only nodding her head while drowning in sorrow. She had no idea what to do, but the truth couldn't come from her mouth. The fact was that she loved Paton so much that giving Haslem that money to keep his mouth shut about a killing that even May didn't know about, including sleeping with him so he could keep his mouth shut, it was all worth it. She couldn't live if she was away from Paton, and she would do what she had to do to make him happy again. The fact that she had to face secretly was that he knew, he knew of her affair. He just wouldn't say it.

"Where them kids?" May asked, quickly changing the subject.

"I left them back at the house with Paton."

"Don't leave them chur'in with no man that been drinkin'." May began walking back into the house, and immediately, Rain stopped crying and started to run. She ran as fast as her feet could carry her until she caught the bus which took her back to the area where she lived. The one person on her mind was her daughter – Jocelyn.

***

Paton sat back in his seat and watched Junior and Jocelyn play on the floor. There was no sound in the house at all except the sound of them making noise with each other, tossing small rocks on the floor to see whose would go further. Paton had gotten himself a bottle of alcohol that he'd hidden where he would hide his money, and he placed it beside his chair as he sat back calmly and watched Jocelyn at play.

Each time she smiled, an overwhelming sense of agony fell upon him as flashbacks of Haslem came directly into his mind. As Junior sat there and played with her, he formed an imaginary gulf between the two children. Junior on one side and Jocelyn on the other, and he didn't want his son to believe a lie.

"That ain't your sister, Junior."

"Sir, daddy?"

"Come here, son."

Junior got up and moved away from Jocelyn who kept playing all by herself. When he reached his father, he jumped up in his lap and watched as he took a sip of whatever was in the bottle. Then, he watched his father's lips move as he asked him a pointed question.

"You think she look like you, Junior?"

Junior shrugged his shoulders. At the tender age of five, he barely knew how to recognize himself, much less the looks of himself in someone else.

"Don't shrug your shoulders at me, boy. Open your mouth and talk," Paton ordered his son who still didn't understand the question, so Paton pushed him back off of his knee and kept drinking. He sat there, growing increasingly disgusted by Jocelyn's presence and the fact that all of what he hated was stored inside her. He was the one feeding her and clothing her and even tuckin' her in at night.

"Daddy, can I come sit on your lap?" Jocelyn asked while Junior went to sit back down. Paton didn't answer. He only stared back at her with drunken eyes and began to hallucinate as she walked toward him. Her childishly, innocent flutter across the room transformed into a menacing, harlot's gait as Jocelyn's childish smile twisted into Haslem's evil grin before his very eyes. Even Jocelyn's hairline matched her true father's, and the texture of her hair was nothing like Paton's nor Rain's. It was his, and to Paton, she was coming to mock him.

He allowed her to climb up onto his lap, and he watched her as she pulled up on his shirt and then his collar to sit down. Her head leaned against his chest, and he started to stare at her like she was something else other than a little girl. The only daughter that he'd ever known started to play with his cheeks like she'd like to do since she was a baby. Paton used to move his face directly in front of hers, place her hands on his cheeks, and make jesting baby noises. This time was different. As Jocelyn played with his cheeks, he continued to examine her as if she was a woman.

"I have to go to the bathroom." She slid off of his leg, and he followed her to the hallway with his eyes. When she turned the corner, he got up from his chair and pat Junior on the top of his head as he followed her down the hall and into the bathroom. Jocelyn turned around and looked at the man she'd known as her father for all her life. She didn't say anything to him, but she didn't undress either. Apparently, she thought he had something to tell her as he leaned on the side of the door frame and waited for her to move toward the toilet.

"Poppa, what's the matter? Why are you at the door? I'm a big girl now, and mama said I can use it all on my own self," she stated proud of herself. "I been not needed anybody to look after me in the bathroom," she bragged.

Paton didn't move. He stood there, still waiting, and then he finally spoke. "Just makin' sure my baby girl's alright. Since you a big girl now... I'll shut the door."

Jocelyn turned around and proceeded to be the big girl that she was and used the bathroom while Paton closed the door until there was nothing left but a small crack. When he looked up and to the left, there was Rain standing with Junior by her side at the other end of the small hallway. They were only ten feet apart, and they stared at each other like strangers. Rain felt relief as she panted from running all the way home with the stress of wondering about the well being of her daughter, while it was Paton who stared back at Rain with a stone face for about three of the longest seconds of Rain's life. Then, he gave her the smile that she was so accustomed to having, walked her way, and then kissed her on her lips.

"Where's Jocie?" she asked him as he backed away from her stiff lips. All the way back home, thoughts raced through her mind about Paton having hid the fight between himself and Haslem. The anxiety rose to a level of panic during the bus ride home, and she could barely breathe just thinking about what Paton could have found out about.

As Paton stood beside her, staring her down from head to toe, the only place Rain concerned herself with was who was down the hallway. A range of emotion bombarded her inner woman because of the unknown, and with the way Paton had been behaving, what May said to her shook her down to the very bones beneath her skin. If she would have known that Paton had a fight with the man whom she hated to lay with but was forced into doing so, she would have never left Jocelyn alone with him out of fear that he would lash out. No matter where or who she came from, Rain loved her first born, and she was to make sure nothing happened to her.

"She just went to the bathroom, Rain. I went to check on her." He walked back to his chair and took his son with him. "She'll be out in a minute."

Rain let out a deep sigh of relief that Paton sensed was a sigh of fear, like Rain must have been afraid for something. He stared down at her hands and she was rubbing them together like she'd just left from walking in chilling cold weather. He smirked a little because he figured that she'd found out about his run in, but he decided to keep the fight with Haslem to himself. He thought it humorous to see her cringe while waiting on the bathroom door to come open. When Jocelyn did come out of the bathroom to spot her mom in the hallway, she ran with the same smile on her face all the way into her mother's arms. It was Paton who watched them embrace as he imagined Haslem holding her just as close to him in order to form Jocie inside his wife's womb.

As Jocelyn looked at her mother, hopeful to show her what she'd been doing while she was gone, she pointed at Paton, her doll, and smiled, causing him to get up and leave out of the house with Junior by his side. When the door shut behind him, Rain rushed into the kitchen to fix him a nice meal. Jocelyn was fine. May was wrong about worrying about her alone with Paton. She was right about one thing though…not telling Paton anything he already knew and just making him feel like the greatest man alive.

There wasn't a night or day that went by that Rain didn't feel the guilt of the unspoken. Each day, she even looked for signs that Paton was mistreating Jocelyn in any way, and she turned up with nothing. After Paton would come back home from job searching or doing an odd job to bring food home, he would play with the children as if there was never a problem outside or inside the house. As a matter of fact, his playing with the children increased while his interaction with her decreased. The children played with him so much until they would even run outside to meet him before he would step foot in the house.

When Paton would come inside, Jocelyn on one leg and Junior on the other, he would move toward Rain and kiss her on the neck. This caused Rain to continue on ignoring whatever happened between him, her and Haslem so that she could focus on making things right. To her, nobody even had to know anything else, and by how things were going, Haslem probably never said too much to Paton at all because Paton never said anything to her. There was just one thing that Rain couldn't put her finger on. It was Paton's drinking at night.

One night, it started as a half a bottle, and that was after he began hitting his chest with a closed fist in the middle of the night while he slept. Rain woke up to the pounding of it, and when she tried to stop his hand, it slammed her wrist into his chest instead. Her scream woke him up, and it was then that he grabbed her by the face with his palm and shoved her onto the bed. Rain's arms were stretched out to the sides as a result of the shock that she was thrown into as she stared into the eyes of what looked like a dead soul. Paton didn't even see her, but he was looking right at her.

After her initial shock, Rain fought to get up, but with one arm, he held her down in place by her face. It was soon enough that she couldn't breathe as he pressed the back of her head down into the cover. Then, she dug her nails into his neck and pulled until she wept through her fear because she loved Paton so much that she didn't want to hurt him purposely. To watch his skin break became the miracle that saved her life because it was only then that life came back to his eyes, and the man she'd laid next to for six years as her husband came back. Paton fell backwards onto the floor and everything appeared foreign as he searched through the wood floor where he kept his stolen money, and it was still no longer there.

From the empty floor, he stared back at Rain with tears in his eyes, and he began to shake his head slowly. What started out as a calm motion escalated to Paton holding his head tightly as he shook it violently, so much so that Rain shuffled to the other side of the bed frightened and screaming. She screamed so loudly that Jocelyn woke up and ran into the room to her mother's side. At the sight of Jocelyn, Paton jerked back against the closet door, banging it so hard that it was a wonder it stayed on the hinges. Quickly, he reached under his mattress and pulled out a small bottle of alcohol and drank it down. Rain then rushed to put Jocelyn back in the bed. She didn't sleep that night, and the drinking got worse, but he'd never attacked her again in that manner, although sometimes Paton would strike her before she put it to an end with a threat of her own. Eventually, he told Rain he had to drink at night to keep demons off of him, so she let him sleep in the living room as he requested. She had to let him because she knew what she'd done, and her guilt plagued her. Still, she kept quiet. In the meantime, the family continued to struggle financially as Paton continued to battle angry demons that he could no longer subdue since he was a child atop the newer and harder demons that came at him seven times stronger as a full grown man.

Paton didn't get his alcohol from Janie all the time, but he always had it available although he had no money to spare. There was only one other person he could bum from and that was his old friend Jesse. Ever since Paton picked up his first bottle at Janie's house, he'd met up with Jesse multiple times, not because he wanted the friendly conversation, but because he began to long for the drink at night. Other things came along with his association with the long and still skinny Jesse, and that was meeting up with a whole new set of people that had the same habit as he did.

Before, when Paton was on a good path for a certain number of years, he only dealt with people mostly of integrity - not because he felt he was above anyone, but because his mom's voice still had a small sound in his ears. She used to repeat those Proverbs of the Holy Bible that her mom made her memorize. There was one that said something like *wise people hear, listen and learn wise instruction, but fools don't like wise instruction at all. The fear of God is the first of all wisdom.* Proverbs was one of the books of the Bible that Sarah needed Paton to know because it talked to men, and she wanted Paton to be a great man. Before she died, he even promised her that he would be, but the more he felt failure, the less he remembered his promise to his mother along with the biblical principle she taught him. After a while, he couldn't stand even looking at Rain when she picked the Bible up because of what he knew about her and what he didn't want to know about himself and his thoughts. Those same thoughts he ended up sharing over some whiskey with his new set of friends eventually.

"I don't know what I'ma do, Jesse. Seem like the world don't wanna do nothin' but swallow me up. Feel like I need to be right there with D.B., my moms and pops. Ain't nothin' here no way 'cept the air to keep you livin', and you can't stop breathin' so you got no choice til your heart stop," Paton complained in a tipsy stupor. His words slurred only slightly as he looked at the last dollar bill in his hand. Then he lifted it up high and ripped it down the middle. "Here take this...we been up together and we down together, but least we together."

Jesse always had liquor streaming somewhere in his bloodstream, therefore, it was easier to get him tipsy but harder to get him to the point where he was completely drunk due to his tolerance level. Where Paton could hold only two before his head would spin, Jesse could hold about six before he started stumbling. Jesse was on his third one. Paton was only on his first.

"And we gon' stay together tonight, ain't we?" he laughed. "Ain't nobody but us stuck in this hole we in. Look around here. Everybody else got work and pay, and we gots nothin'." Then he held up the ripped half of dollar Paton gave him. "We can't even spend this 'cause it ain't even a real fifty cent piece!" he hollered as he laughed hysterically. Jesse's long leg accidentally kicked over the last bit of joy juice they had left, and it emptied out all over the patchy grass.

"We coulda' sold that," Paton laughed along with him as he proceeded to rip up the half dollar bill that was in his hand. "I got a good idea, Jesse. Let's go get some money." Paton's face grew to a seriousness that would cause anyone to think he hadn't had a bit of rum.

"How you say we gon' do that?"

Paton stood up and looked into the night sky. "I know an address of somebody that owe me...and ain't got no choice but to give it to me when I come get it." He shot a glance at Jesse so stern that even he nearly sobered up. "He been holdin' it for me, case I need something. It's payback," Paton continued.

"Where you gon' get money from this late?"

"You comin'?" he asked Jesse. "Lest I can go and get it myself. I just want some company on the way." He watched as Jesse carefully pulled himself up from the railing shaking his head in disagreement, having a bad feeling about Paton's sudden change in tone. At that, Paton took a playful jab at him on the shoulder. "Come on, man. We ain't been nowhere together in a long time," Paton joked, calming the tension down.

"Aw'right. Let's go. Ain't nothing else to do." Jesse turned around, picked up a small rock and tossed it at the front door to alert his mom that he was leaving the front, however, it missed the door. Then, they both walked off into the night.

"How far away is this money you got to get?"

"We gone take a short cut, Jesse. Right round the back, pass my house on down a little ways, and we'll get there. We got all night. What's the rush?"

"Ain't your old lady gone be looking for you?"

"I told her I was gonna be out late. Her and the ch..." he paused before completing the word children. "She gone to bed."

"You and Rain lookin' to make some mo' babies? You been on it back to back…"

"Ain't no mo'." Paton interrupted. "That's enough for now…maybe even forever." The conversation created a new level of irritation for Paton, but he pretended that the line of questioning didn't bother him by answering with a good excuse. "Got no money, Jesse. How I'm supposed to have a bigger family than that with no money? Only a fool would keep breedin' with no feedin'."

"I ain't never had nothin'. Nothing but my bottle, myself, and my mama. If she gone, I'm gone. That's the way I see it." Jesse jumbled his words as he continued talking beyond the point where Paton halted listening. Instead, Paton wondered if it was a good idea to bring him along.

Before he even left his own home, Paton established the idea of going back for his money after he got the address from a stranger who happened to know Haslem. That was where the rest of his money went; he paid the unknown man to keep quiet and give him the directions. It turned out that Haslem lived in the opposite direction as Janie, and in the same distance. It would be an average walk, but he was willing to do it in the middle of the night so that no one would suspect him going.

The time was about one o'clock in the morning when he and Jesse got to what appeared to be the house Paton waited all day long to find. As he walked toward the house from the street, the red front door that the stranger told him about stood out clearly, and while Jesse still had no clue about what was going on, Paton quickly turned onto the walkway up the front door.

"This the house?"

"Yeah," Paton answered.

"Don't look much like he got more than us," he grinned.

"He don't, but he owe me. I got to go 'round back. He left the door open for me. Just sit down here," Paton ordered, pointing to the cement walkway outside the front door while he wiped the sweat from his face. "I'll be back 'round front with the money in a minute."

Jesse didn't hesitate on doing what he said because one thing Paton already figured out was that Jesse would follow anyone anywhere for liquor money. He would believe anything and say anything to get it, but he would only go so far. What Paton was doing was one of those things that Jesse would have never gone for a day in his life. He may have been an alcoholic, but there wasn't a mean bone in his body that was cut to do anybody wrong purposely.

As Paton walked confidently out of Jesse's sight, he slowed to a creeping gait when he reached the back of the house. There was uncut grass and bushes all around the dingy property, and it smelled of a stench that Paton couldn't identify. Although the property was small, there were two back windows and a back door, all of which Paton would try to enter into as quietly as he could.

Because of the darkness, Paton couldn't see inside the first window as he inched as closely as he could to it. As he walked to the back door, it was locked, but as he felt at the side of the house, a bit closer to the other window, his finger went inside. The second window was ajar. Before opening the window the rest of the way so that he could climb in, he placed his ear up to the corner of the opening and listened. It was Haslem's room. He knew it because there was an unseen man inside breathing so hard that he was snoring, and Paton didn't waste any more time.

Just in case the window made any noise, he slid it up in one fast push. The window was low enough for Paton to lift one leg up over the sill and slide inside. Once inside, however, he couldn't see anything. He became blind, and there was no help from the moon or the stars because of the high bush and trees behind the house. Paton stood tall and shut his eyes, his blood pressure elevating and his heart pounding, not out of fear of any man, woman or beast, but because the man who took his money and wife slept before him without a care in the world.

He followed the breathing, which wasn't far from the window at all. When he felt the edge of what he thought was a bed, he leaned over slowly until he felt the breath of Haslem on his cheek. Then, he realized that he wasn't on a bed, but a chair that was leaned back onto a wall. Paton felt the edges of the chair, and even the legs where they stopped. He carefully rubbed his fingers to the head rest, and when he finally knew how Haslem would fall back, he moved within centimeters to his face, placed his left hand above his mouth without touching it and then finally grabbed Haslem by his throat, slamming him down on to the floor along with the chair he slept in.

Haslem didn't know what happened until he felt a hand cover his mouth and a grip so tight on his neck that he thought he was going to die for sure. Paton's eyes stared down into the darkness, and he kept a firm grip on Haslem's neck and mouth until the faintest outline of the man he grew to hate came into focus.

"This you, ain't it? What's your name?" he asked removing his hand, "And if you yell one bit, I kill ya'. Pop your neck like you a little doll baby."

Instead of answering, Haslem attempted to fight back but couldn't because his body was bent down and trapped between the chair and Paton's terrible strength.

"Get out my house!" Haslem struggled.

"This here ain't yo' house. Now I said, name yo'self." The sweat dripped down onto Paton's hand as it poured from his head. "Answer me!"

"Haslem! Haslem! What I done to you? What I done?" he yelled, shaken in fear by someone standing over him that he couldn't even see to identify. Haslem's arms gripped Paton's arms forcefully, trying with all his might to remove Paton's hands from his neck. His efforts fail as his strength began to weaken against an enraged Paton.

"Gimme my money! I want it all! Give it to me!" Paton lifted his hand, punched him in his face, and then placed both hands on his neck, squeezing until he heard him gasp.

"I ain't got it! You killin' me, Paton."

"Oh, you know me, huh? I'm the only one you done stole from? Ain't no way you spent all that money. Ain't no way!"

"I ain't workin, Paton. Please...I'm tellin' the truth. I ain't workin'...ain't worked in months. The money gone, all of it."

Paton looked down at him in disbelief. "Find it!" he hollered, his voice coming to a raging growl. "You find my money tonight," he warned as he quieted down, "Or I'ma kill you. You hear that? This gone be your last night breathing." He squeezed his neck tighter, and no matter what Haslem did or how he struggled to talk and fight away from Paton's grip, it was too late. Paton had already gone from asking for his money to only focusing on destroying the future of the man who succeeded in destroying his.

Paton squeezed and shook his neck until he felt the force of Haslem's fingertips against his arms loosen and his body grow limp. Even then, he failed to let go completely. Paton lifted him up from the ground by his neck, and then promised the dead man one thing as his head fell backwards.

"I'm gonna get my money, and I'm gonna get my life back from you." Then, he shook his neck as if he wanted to snap it in two. "On your blood…on your blood," he stressed. "I'll kill every piece of you until you're gone from here forever. You hear me?" Paton's lips coiled around themselves, and his teeth grinded together as the breath from his nostrils came out like a raging bull. Then, he changed in the blink of an eye. All of his anger changed into a deep, dark sadness, and he cried, "I can't help it, you see this? I can't let you leave me here like this, with nothing. I ain't got nothing…" After staring into the darkness, he suddenly dried his eyes, cleared his throat and then, with full force, threw Haslem's head against the wall.

He began to frantically search for money in the dark. Paton rubbed his hand on the sides of Haslem at his pockets, but there wasn't a wallet or money inside his pocket. Then, he moved toward what felt like a dresser and started searching with his fingers until he ran his hand across some rolled coins, a small box full, and underneath it was something that felt like dollars, but only a couple. Stumbling over something unidentified on the floor, Paton went back to the window and climbed out with the money he found in his hand.

"Yeah, got my money," he said to himself as he bolted from the side of the house, but then, he stopped. He stared at Jesse still sitting on the porch of the house, and before he showed his face, he contemplated walking back home alone, to leave Jesse sitting right there.

Paton looked around behind himself. There were other homes, but none that could have seen him enter Haslem's house or come out. There was too much foliage. He looked down at the money he craved to have again, even if it was just a little bit. Then, he crept closer to look back at Jesse again, and he thought about how Jesse didn't really need anything. How he had no life, and besides that, it was Jesse who was the only other person who knew he was here. If he got too tipsy from here on out after Haslem's body was found, people would start questioning things, and Jesse was liable to talk. Paton knew he needed an alibi. His alibi more than likely wouldn't come by Jesse's tongue. Paton knew this because Jesse had already run his mouth too much in his drunkenness about the fire that Paton set a long time ago. How much more would he run his mouth about this?

His only choice would be to use Janie. In a split second decision, he returned to the back side of the house out of breath, looking all around himself for a way out of the situation he just created. While his heart seemed to skip beats as a result of the adrenaline pumping through his body, he searched for an escape around him. The only way he could get away without Jesse was to take a dark patch of land that he'd never taken before, meaning that he wouldn't know what was on the other side. He slowly walked back to look at a clueless Jesse on the front side of the house, and without giving himself more time to think anything through, he left him there. He ran with the money in hand, the entire time thinking about Jesse and how he would make it to Janie's house just in time to make her his alibi. However, he stopped in his tracks about eighty feet from where he killed Haslem. Making a full turn to face the house again, he doubled back to the place where he began.

"Come on, Jesse, let's go." Paton didn't even stop walking to wait on him to catch up. He tried to play calm, but his legs wouldn't let him. "Come on, man."

"What took so long though? How much money in that box?"

"Enough. He owed me some dimes. I'll give you some rolls when we get to the house. We just gotta get down the road."

"Why you rushin'?" When Paton didn't answer, Jesse caught up to him and repeated himself. "Wait up, man. Why you just about runnin'? We got a long ways to walk, and ain't no stores open no way."

Paton stopped to face Jesse as they turned the corner, about to head out through a short cut. As Paton stared around the area, doing his best to not disturb the silence, he spoke. "Look here. I need to you to be as quiet as a mouse while we walkin' out here," he warned. "I did something back there, Jesse. Before you say anything, I needed the money. It ain't a lot, but it's money…and I ain't going into no detail either. Let's just get outta here fast." He turned to walk away, but Jesse quickly sobered up from his small buzz and grabbed Paton's shirt, nearly ripping it.

"What you do?" Jesse asked, yanking Paton closer. "What the hell did you do?" he stressed fearfully. His whole body got the shakes, and Paton snatched Jesse's hand away from his clothing.

"You said you needed money right? Me and you, so I got it…and you went with me."

"Me?" Jesse shouted back. "You set me up for whatever you did back there?"

"Set you up? Set you up is what you think I did? Naw," Paton strained as he held his voice at a minimum. "I ain't set you up, but I coulda'. This time, I kept you from settin' me up." He stepped right up to a frozen Jesse, and continued. "You see how you always be making mention of me and that fire I set back when Drowning Boy died?" Paton's eyes glossed in the night while underneath the trees, and he spoke like a man that had no turning back in sight. This was what frightened Jesse the most as he recalled how Paton killed once before that he knew of, and he didn't want to be the next.

"Make mention of the fire?" Jesse pretended to have shunned the memory a long time ago, but Paton knew better.

"See how you was out there talkin' about it and about to tell my girl before she became my wife? 'Member that...'cause I sho' do? Now...say somethin' else. If I go down, you goin', too, after they find that man body dead in his house later."

"You kill him, Pate? Oh Jesus!" Jesse turned around in circles looking for a way out, but Paton only stood there and watched how lost he'd gotten behind his words. That was when he knew that Jesse wasn't going to say a thing about it. He was too afraid.

"I got us this money, and we gonna go back on that porch of yours and make plenty noise so folk will see us out there, including your mom. We ain't getting caught less you say it, and you'll be squealing on your own self then. You get what I'm sayin'? Huh?" he asked, expecting a fast, affirmative answer.

Jesse only held out his arms like he was heaving a heavy load in front of him. His mouth was dropped open as the obvious chaos he'd gotten involved in flowed through his mind, but the words to express his disgust wouldn't come out. He drove a look into Paton as if he never knew him, like he wasn't the same man he grew up with so long ago.

"What you doin' this to me for, Pate? I ain't got nothin'. I be to myself every day, and I got…"

Paton cut his sentence short, "You got nothing to worry 'bout…long as you keep your mouth shut. Now we got to go, and don't you never think that I trusts you. So I'll be watching."

Quietly and weakly, Jesse responded, "But you owe me. You owe me because I ain't never went to no police about nothin'.'

"No, you owe me!" he shouted, louder than he wanted to, but his emotions got the most of him. "It was you who ran out there in them woods and just watched. You ain't even help me! If they'd a shot both of us, all your weak ass woulda' done was run." Paton then spits onto the ground. "That's how much I think about what I owe you. No…you still owe me," he stated, pointing at Jesse's face. "Everybody 'round here owes me, but ain't nobody payin' up. So, I'm takin'. I ain't standin' around here cryin' like you are though," he stated, antagonizing a poor Jesse who only wanted to keep to himself and mind his own business. Unfortunately, he'd ended up caught up again in one of Paton's bad affairs, and he watched as Paton started pushing forward toward his house. He had no choice but to follow behind and continue on with his newfound enemy's plan.

Paton didn't care if Jesse followed behind him closely or not. What he did care about was that Jesse remained frightened, so much so that it was almost certain that he would never reveal anything that happened that night or any other night. Paton was serious, and he felt that Jesse should have chosen sides a long time ago. It was always in the back of Paton's mind, but it was this particular night that he made it known in the worst way by setting Jesse up in the worst way. It was Paton's way of getting back what was taken from him monetarily and soon, in every other way.

As they came within a few feet of Jesse's home, Paton slowed down to allow Jesse to catch up to him. He had to ask him something. It was something that had been on his mind for a while, but he didn't act on it. He stared down into the box, and counted the small amount of rolled coins laying inside. It wasn't a third or even a fourth of the money he'd saved, including the couple of dollars he took. Paton had already made up his mind.

"How many them guys that be with you married, Jesse?"

Having already given up, he pitifully answered, "Most of 'em."

"Get 'em together for me, so I can spot 'em."

"Spot 'em for what, Pate? I ain't gettin' involved!"

Paton dropped the box of money on the ground and manhandled the tall Jesse like he was beneath him. "Now, you look here. You ain't got no choice. I'm going back home after this, but before that, you about to list me the names of them married men who throw the bottle back just like you do and worse. Don't want no single ones yet. Just the married ones. Then, I'll let you on your way, Jesse," he smiled. "Keep them coins." Then he shoved the dollars into his pocket and went to sit on Jesse's porch, fixing his pants legs and leaning back onto the rail like he'd been there all the time. Jesse only walked back to his porch, slumped over after picking up the box of coins from the ground.

Jesse needed a drink, and Paton knew it. His old friend that he just took complete control over was lost in the darkness, not knowing what he needed to do first. Therefore, Paton guided him further.

"You need to go on in the house and put that box underneath your bed or something…so your mom can hear you out here. If she sleep, you need to make some noise," Paton instructed. "Don't think about sayin' one thing. Sober up."

"Paton, this drink done made you crazy or something, man. What's wrong with you? It ain't got to be like this."

"Ain't never had to be like nothin'." Paton stated, finding a half of cigar on the ground. He picked it up, wiped it off and then lit it with a match he had in his pocket. "It just is…now ain't that right?" He put the cigar in his mouth while Jesse walked on inside the house.

As Paton sat on the porch, he didn't feel one ounce of regret as he recalled the events that happened just prior to him taking back what he felt rightfully belonged to him, including full possession of his wife. With Haslem gone, he no longer had to live with the thought of being made ashamed of what Rain was doing or ever did behind his back. What man couldn't keep control of his house? They would call him weak with a whore for a wife, and he wasn't about to let that fall onto his head. The only thing left he had to do was earn all the money back that he ever lost, and just like he told Haslem, he would do it off his blood. Paton meant every word.

"Paton, don't you think you need to go on home now? Jesse 'bout tired and need his rest. He don't look too good. Get on off my porch," Jesse's mom called from the inside of the house. Paton didn't move. The last thing he was gonna do was leave Jesse while his mom was awake, so he waited for Jesse to come back to the door. Instead, Jesse's mother crept to the door before he got there.

"I said I want you out from 'round here. I could tell it since way back. You troubled…and a double minded man is unstable in all his ways. You ain't takin' Jesse no further with you…"

"Ma!" Paton heard Jesse call from the back of the dark house while he didn't pay his mother any attention. Paton only cracked a smile as he chewed on the end of the cigar while Jesse's mom stared him down.

"You used to be a good boy, Paton. My eyes never lied to me. I see evil in you. It done festered…"

"Ma! Go on back indoors. Me and Paton just sittin' out here is all. He'll be gone soon enough."

"I want him gone, Jesse," she stated, not moving Paton from her line of vision. "That man ain't no boy no more. Where you stuck, he ain't. He the cause of you like you is now because I hear you in the night." She looked at her son. "You can't be that blind that you can't see it. He done always leaded y'all wrong, and you still lettin' him do it."

"I ain't got no control over nobody, ma'am. Jesse do what Jesse wanna do." Paton stood up from the porch and wiped his pants clean. "Jesse say what he wanna say, too. Another man can't make another man do nothing, even if that man gotta die."

Jesse's eyes buckled at the man who he once used to run with, without having a care to look over his shoulder. They'd always had a pact to watch out for each other, even in the worst of times. Never once did Jesse think that Paton would set him up, but it was far too late to turn back now, despite his mother's warnings.

"Come on, Paton," Jesse stated, moving his mother back some before he closed the door, giving her a kiss in the process. When he placed one foot on the steps, he glared his hardest at Paton because he loved his mom, and the death threat that he shot out wasn't something that Jesse took lightly. "You planning on killin' me? You that much out your mind you would kill me, after all this?"

"Forget the list. Set up something like you usually do, and I'll take care of the rest. That man back there dead, and I don't care if the police come, keep your mouth quiet." Paton then walked off, dragging his feet against the ground, like the adrenaline he once had dissipated, allowing the alcohol he drank to take back over. He arrived back to his home in the early hours of the morning, and Rain was still in the bed asleep.

"Hey there, little baby girl. It's me…your daddy," he whispered into Jocelyn's ear as she slept soundly in the bed. Rain didn't realize he'd come in the house already, and Paton didn't want her to know. When he walked inside, the first place he went was to Jocelyn's small room and shut the door. Before he even spoke to her, he stood silently in the doorway and stared into the black of night, listening to her breathe. It sounded foreign to him, not like the little girl he once knew. There was a sound of betrayal that mingled inside her, and each time it came out, it bothered him more and more. Still he wanted her to believe he loved her, in order to get her to do what he wanted her to do.

"Poppa?

"Yeah, baby girl?" When he spoke to her, he flashed back to only an hour or so ago when he strangled her real father to death. When his eyes met Jocelyn's, he thought he could still see Haslem, torturing him over and over again by having the upper hand in his household even though he was dead.

"You stayin' in here now, Poppa, or are you leaving again like you did before?"

"You want me to stay in here with you?"

"Yeah, and tell me a story like you do all the time. Tell me the one about the goose and the chicken, Poppa, please!" she asked, excited because she hadn't seen the man she knew as her father since she went to bed at seven o'clock, which was early for her because she wasn't feeling well. She missed his story time this particular night.

"I got a new story for you, so scoot over," he told her while taking off his shoes before climbing into the bed, "and sit over here on my lap. I'm gonna tell you 'bout a special little girl who got everything in the world because she was daddy's little girl, and she learned everything he taught her. Are you that girl?"

"Yessir," she responded, rubbing her eyes. Obviously, still tired and struggling to stay up with the only father she'd ever known. "I'm the best baby girl ever! That's what you say, ain't it?"

"Yes ma'am. And you just turned into a bigger girl."

"I did? That fast?"

"Yep. And there's some other things that big girls have to do in order to stay big girls."

"What...tell me!"

"Shh." He put his hand up to her lips, and then he rubbed them from side to side. Then he removed them. "You have to learn to keep secrets, and whatever any girl's father tells her to do, she can't tell anybody. That there is what big girls do, and they grow up to be the best women, just like your momma."

"I'm gonna be like momma? That shole is good because I love momma," she whispered, nodding her head up and down.

Paton paused before answering. "Big girls love they daddy's more. Your momma can't teach you what I can. Now, give your daddy a kiss right here," he said pointing to his cheek, "And then you lay down here with me and go to sleep."

"Goodnight, daddy," she said happily, kissed him on his cheek, and then laid down to go back to sleep. Paton laid down, too, making this the beginning of his training of Jocelyn into the woman he wanted her to become; a woman that could make all the money that Haslem stole while he forced Rain on her back through blackmail.

Paton didn't do anything to her but lay there with his hand on her until she went to sleep. He wanted her to get used to having a man lay with her in a bed, particularly him. Before she even woke back up, Paton had already left and slid into the bed with Rain. Paton had formed a huge disconnect between his wife and her daughter, Jocelyn, in his mind. Where he planned to torture one, he planned to regain the other, who he felt should have only been his all along with his wedding vows.

He turned Rain over, and although she was tired, she already knew what he wanted. The problem was that she didn't want him like she used to want him. Ever since she believed he found out something about her, the way he made love to her didn't feel as special as it used to feel. Instead, she always felt like she was being raped, almost the same way she would feel with Haslem. She didn't feel his love, and in turn, she couldn't feel anything. She lived with that absence while continuing to please him. There was something different when he turned her over that night, however, and she felt it in the way he touched her, even in how he kissed her face. It was like he'd found something that he'd lost for a very long time.

Paton placed his hand on her face, the same hands that he'd used to murder the man who, in his eyes, hunted her down and stole the only woman he'd ever loved. He rubbed her cheek like it was a delicate flower petal, and he kissed her eyes like they were the most sensitive parts of her body. In the same way he kissed her face, he kissed her neck and then her shoulders. As he undraped her chest, he began to smell the skin on her chest and loved her breasts in ways that he hadn't loved them in a long time.

Wet drops began to fall from his face that didn't feel to Rain like the moisture of sweat, but instead, like tears. Her emotions raced to find out what was wrong, but before she could reach out to him, he caught her hand in mid-motion. Then, he laid it back down on the pillow while he shook his head in a plea for her not to move. Rain didn't fight back although she was torn between her confusion of the moment and feeling his love after such a long time in the same touch.

Paton wept as he licked her from her thighs down to her ankles, lifting her legs high so he wouldn't miss a spot. She was all he ever cared about, the only woman that he ever thought about since the first time he saw her. The anger that he used to make love to her with was finally dead with Haslem, and he had her all to himself once again. As he entered into her, however, there was still that anger that he misplaced, with a smile that he would have to see forever but with a promise that he made a dying Haslem. With his blood, he would take back what was stolen. Jocelyn had become the one he would deceive and destroy in order to wipe her real dad's smile from her face for good. He prepared to trade the bloodline of Haslem's happiness for the sadness that Haslem gave him. The same way Rain hid it from him was to be the same way he hid it from her, not to hurt but to fix everything that went wrong. That was how Paton rationalized their relationship in his head each and every time he and Rain got closer and closer. He understood her love for him and why she did what she did, and it was up to her to understand his love...no matter what.

The next day, Rain left early to go pick some free food from the midwife's garden. There wasn't any money to spare for anything, so whenever she could go to the garden and get some collard greens, tomatoes and corn she would. On the way back home, she would sneak plums and peaches from the trees of some folks that she didn't even know, but she doubted that they paid her any attention. It was while she was at the midwife's house that she heard the news that brought her tomato picking to a halt.

"Rain, you hear 'bout that killin' over there on the other side of town, clear cross on the other side of the creek?"

"Somebody was killed? Around here?" Rain asked, as she tossed the long tomato vine to the side to pick a big, red juicy one from the back.

"They say the man was found near 'bout upside down in his own room. Say 'bout it happened in the middle of the night, but ain't nobody see nothing but a shadow running back behind the house. Say they think the shadow they saw was who done it. Far as I know, they ain't catch the man yet either."

"Well, who was it that got killed?" Rain asked, tucking the tomato she just picked into her bag. She then started picking another tomato off the vine until she heard the name of the man soar out of the midwife's mouth.

"Say it was a man name Haslem. Say he was well known to some on that side. Lived alone, but funny thing is they say he went from poor to rich in a day. Say he fell on some money, but now that he dead, they bettin' on they life he got that money the wrong way. Say he went through it like he didn't work for it, like it didn't 'long to him in the first place. They sayin' whoever kill him, did it lookin' for they money."

Rain dropped the tomato on the ground, and the midwife rushed to pick it back up. "Don't go bruisin' up the food, now. Them children I took out you don't want no soft, mushy fruits. Here." She noticed Rain getting nervous as she gave her back the tomato. "Chile, what's wrong with you? You feelin' fine?"

Startled by the question, Rain hurried to answer. "Yes ma'am, I feel fine. Got a bit dizzy though," she lied as her eyes fell back toward the ground. With her basket half full, she thanked the midwife for once again allowing her to pull from her garden, and started to walk away quickly. "I think I need to go. I'm not feeling too good."

"Well, don't run off. Your basket not filled up, and if you dizzy, you need somethin' to eat. I got a pot of beans on…"

"No ma'am. I have to get going. I'll be back at the end of the week, if you don't mind."

"Alright there. Slow down!" she shouted behind Rain who was already a good twenty feet away, and she continued to increase the distance between them at a great rate of speed.

When the midwife was out of Rain's sight, she ducked behind a tree and sank to the ground. The tomatoes rolled out of the bag as Rain found it difficult to catch her breath. She was having a panic attack as she thought about how Paton wept as he made love to her like it was their very first time. Rain's hands dug into the ground as she thought about how Paton was out the same night that Haslem was killed and how the midwife said it may have been over money, and she vomited, just missing the tomatoes that fell all over the ground.

Her breathing was erratic, and although she hated to sleep with Haslem almost every single week until he took the money, she didn't know how to handle the freedom that she'd just acquired, especially since in her heart of hearts she knew who'd killed him. It was Paton. Rain didn't have to ask, nor did she have to see it with her own eyes. It was the way Paton was that night that told her everything.

Without more delay, she stood up from the ground, wiped her tears away and smiled. She smiled for the first time at the thought of Haslem's name. All before then, there was never a warm welcome or a hello greeting between them. It was always sorrow and fear mixed with a man who knew too much about her while taking advantage of it, even after she got married.

The tomatoes had already ceased from rolling on the ground, and Rain rushed to gather them together so she could get home. Her joy caused her to not feel any remorse for

Haslem, and she finally felt free from having to watch constantly to cover the fact that only she and Haslem knew for the longest time – that Jocelyn, her baby girl, was his and not Paton's. However Paton killed him, she was glad. Every organ inside her body felt free from Haslem's touch, and she would never have to tell Paton up front that Jocelyn wasn't his daughter because there was no one alive to debate it. She finally had her family back…and her life…and getting back home couldn't have been soon enough.

"Junior, go on out back and play for a minute. Wait on Jocie back there. She comin', too."

"Okay, poppa!" Junior shouted and ran outside to play. This left Paton alone with Jocelyn. She wasn't in the living room where he was located, but instead, in her bedroom playing with dolls like she normally did. She would like to set up her dolls like they were all having tea or talking to each other like she would see her mom do at church with the ladies. They hardly ever carried on conversations with her, so she would always listen and repeat some of the things that would say.

"Sista Mary, you got on a nice dress," Jocelyn sang as she flipped her twisted hair behind her back pretending to have on a wig. "And you know what, Sista Dora, what I heard about your new car was right fine!" Jocelyn sang again until she heard her father at her room door. "Poppa, you coming to play with me?"

"If you want me to play, I will."

"Yeah, come on. You sit right here." She pointed to a small, empty spot beside her bed where she thought her father could sit down, but he was far too big a man for that small area. Therefore, he walked in and stooped next to her.

"I think I can fit here just fine. What's this you playin'?"

"Playin' church," she answered matter of factly.

"I'll be the man. What you say?"

"Okay…because somebody need a husband, ain't it, Poppa?"

"I reckon so. You want to see how a man and a girl supposed to do so you can play right?"

"How's that?"

"Come here let me show you how." He picked up a doll baby and brought her close. "Now this is a big girl like you, and all big girls have to learn this way." Then he lifted the doll to his lips, and with his eyes steady on Jocelyn, kissed the doll on the mouth quickly. "Once little girls learn that, they can be big girls like you."

"But, Poppa?" she interrupted confused. "You said I'm a big girl, and I ain't never done nothing like that before."

"Come here. Kiss me right here," he said as he pointed to his cheek. When Jocelyn came over to him, excited that she was finally doing what she was told big girls do, she kissed him right where his finger was. Before she could move, he then kissed her quickly on her lips. "See, now that wasn't too bad, was it?"

"Nope," she answered walking back to her spot while wiping her lips off. "Am I supposed to do that now?"

"Only in secret. All big girls do it in secret, and they never tell."

"Even momma did that, too?" she asked curiously.

Paton thought about all the things Rain did in secret, and responded, "Yeah, even your momma." Just then, Paton heard the door open. "It's time for you to go out and play with Junior. You can take your dolls out."

"Okay. You get two, and I get two." That was when Jocelyn raced outside, but before she got there, she saw her mom and jumped to hug her neck. "Ma, Junior's out back. Come back to play with us." She picked her dolls back up and ran out the door. Rain nodded her head, and when she looked back up, there was Paton.

They stared at each other like it was their first time ever meeting, but there were obvious questions that were to only be answered by a silent tension between them. Rain took off her straw hat that she used to keep her hair and face shielded from the sun as she picked at the garden. Her eyes released tears simultaneously, and they rolled down her face as if in a race. It was Paton that stared at her with a face of stone, innately knowing what her tears were about. He could smell the relief in her face, but he didn't force her to say a word by asking the obvious. Instead, he just looked at her for a few more seconds before retiring into his bedroom, shutting the door behind him. Rain, once the door went completely shut, she collapsed in tears on the floor, repeating the words thank you in a whisper over and over again until her knees began to hurt on the hardwood floor.

Inside the bedroom, Paton moved over to the window where he could keep an eye on the children, his child and Haslem's. His main focus on Haslem's. He rubbed his tongue against his teeth, and sat on the window sill, watching as Junior ran around and knocked her dolls down in the dirt while she fussed.

"Hey, Jocie. Here, baby girl. Come to the window and get these other two dolls," Paton called. Jocelyn ran toward the window at her father's call and jumped up for the dolls since he was holding them higher than her head purposely. He admired her in ways that a man shouldn't admire a child as she jumped, and he lifted his arm higher and higher so she had to strain to touch the very bottom of the dolls' feet. Continuing to taunt her, he allowed one of the dolls to drop from his hand, and surprising to him, she caught it.

"Got it! I got it, see," she laughed. "I got it...now!" she continued, feeling like the big girl that Paton told her she was.

"I see you got it, Jocie. I see. Come gimme some sugar." Paton leaned over and kissed her right on the lips, and Jocelyn, being confident and proud of being a big girl, gave him a kiss back on the lips, thinking nothing of it. Then, Paton gave her the other doll back.

"Thank you, Poppa!" Jocelyn kept playing as Paton studied her more than he'd ever studied her in her life, and each time she smiled, he was reminded of the man who uprooted his home. He became even more determined to get back what Haslem stole from him at all costs. His determination began to soon eat at him until the day he met with Jesse again at a card game in a cut back behind his house where he invited the rest of the fellas.

There were six men that decided to come and play cards, get drunk and have what they considered a good ole time with Jesse. Among the six was Paton, and he had a beer in his hand already. What he didn't plan on doing was drinking it. Being that Paton was such a hard man to read, especially at this particular time in his life, no one knew that something was eating away at his soul. Therefore, they always attributed his mood to his empty wallet, and he would agree to hide the one true fact…he'd learned to hate Jocelyn because of his hatred of Haslem. Killing him wasn't enough to satisfy what he considered the death of his family, so he had a plan.

"What it is y'all 'bout to play?" Paton asked, leaning forward with the beer in his hand. He hadn't drank anything yet, but everyone else was on their second or third round. These men were the worst of the worst, especially when they were away from their families. They'd done, and still do, some of everything like making two and three other families outside of their main one, sleeping with a multitude of women, and the list went on. The one thing all of them did, however, was keep jobs which was hard for Paton and Jesse to do. Where there was a man with a job, there was money, easy money.

"We 'bout to play Gin Rummy," one of the men answered while taking a sip of his drink and shuffling the cards. Jesse sat back and shot glances at Paton every two minutes, not knowing what he was setting up. Whatever it was, he wanted no more parts of it. Jesse was so scared, he hadn't taken too many sips of his own alcohol which was odd.

"Gin Rummy, huh? Lemme sit back and watch you deal. I go next game," Paton responded as he pat the heel of his shoe in the ground directly on top of an ant mound. He watched the ants scatter everywhere, and instead of getting up from his seat, he allowed them to crawl in order to stomp them all to death as he sat there under the leaves of a lowering tree. Then, his eyes met Jesse's. As he stared back at him, he continued to bang his foot into the ground which turned out to be a warning from Jesse's vantage point. Quickly, Jesse turned back around to face the game.

"Anybody want some more liquor? It's on me," Jesse lied. Paton purchased the liquor with all the money he had left in order to get them to agree to something they may not agree to in their right mind without a bit of coaxing.

"Yeah, Jesse, go ahead and bring out the rest. That's a good idea, man. Get it right out here!" Paton stated, sounding excited, but not for the right reasons. Him sending Jesse in for more drinks was a set up so that he could ask the men in private about their feelings on sex with other women. He leaned back in his chair and chose the three out of four men that he felt he could talk into it.

"How many of y'all done tasted something foreign other than your wife?" He didn't even wait on them to answer but answered it for them. "Good, ain't it? Almost the best it is, huh?"

"Hell yeah, Paton. What you talkin' 'bout? I had this beautiful lady on me one time, boy," he sang in a high pitch, "And she was a red bone and hot as a firecracker, too. When wife wasn't there, she was, and I did what I had to do."

"Ever had a young thang?" Paton asked.

"No, man...don't mess with that none. I keep mine close to my age. I got three of 'em now, and when I don't go home, their doors are always open for me."

"Yeah, me too. I got one always waitin' on me, and I can't seem to let her go. I try," he laughed, "but she do things to me that just ain't possible by no regular woman!"

The men started laughing as one of them dealt, but two of the men sat without uttering a word. One of them looked directly at Paton and hesitated a grin before his mouth went back to a serious state. Paton then leaned forward and cocked his head to the side, continuing to look at him. Then, he noticed the man's nervousness that caused a small bead of sweat to come from his forehead. That was when he knew that he was the one due to the nervousness he exuded.

After Paton finally got his chance to play and earned his loss at Gin Rummy, he went over to stand next to the man who struck him as uneasy at his question.

"So tell me somethin'," Paton started with a swig of his drink, pretending to take more down than what he actually did. He needed his wit about him to control the situation he was about to start as he decided to take a seat on the stomp of a tree.

"What's that, Pate?" the man answered nervously.

As soon as Paton heard his question, the most perverse words he'd ever spoken in his life came from his mouth. "How young you like 'em?" The whole time he spoke, Paton was thinking about Jocelyn.

"What you mean?" the man avoided.

"You heard me, and you know what I mean. Tell you what..." Paton stated, standing up to face him so no one could read his lips and barely hear his voice. "Loan me your address in my ear, and I'll bring a young thang by for you. It costs though, and it's secret. We keep this in house. One go down, we all go down. Already tradin' off with a couple right now, been doing it for six months," he lied to make the man feel more at ease. "She young and can be trained for whatever."

The man's eyes shifted over to the other men. "Any of them know?"

"No, man. Whoever I talk to know, and ain't no hearsay. I'm the one that do the talking, nobody else. Nobody talks about it with nobody. Just me." Paton's eyes followed the eyes of the hesitant customer, and then warned him to stop looking over there. "Act easy. Ain't nothing. She real young. You got yourself a record?"

Immediately, the man's focus jumped from the card game and back to Paton. "Near 'bout...can't prove nothing, so I didn't get no time."

"But you done been in trouble before?"

"Yeah," he nodded.

That was the right answer for Paton. He wanted men with something to lose, like their freedom, because if a man had something to lose, he could keep a ton of secrets over being locked up behind bars.

"Like I said, lend me that address, and have a stack of money for me."

The conversation continued, and Paton even discussed the age of Jocelyn, although, never telling the man that it was his daughter. In every aspect, the discussion was rooted in the pits of hatred and hell, but at that point, Paton didn't care. The more he talked about it, the more he drank until the deal was made. Paton would end up taking the only daughter that he'd ever known to meet the strange man in two weeks, and that money would be the fastest way to collect the debt that Haslem died owing.

Two weeks came very slowly. Paton had become low on money, a bit too low, and every time he had to go to bed hungry and jobless, the more he visited Jocelyn in her room. Rain had already gone to work at a new place part time, and that left him alone with Jocelyn and Junior.

Usually, after Paton would get Junior out of his hair, he would approach Jocelyn, who would be doing all the things a young, innocent girl did. She was a bright little ray of sunshine, and it was obvious that she wanted long flowing hair down her back by the way she would toss her twists to and fro. Her hair already touched her shoulders, but it wasn't long enough for her. She would always beg her mom to put the twists further down at the back part of her head so her hair could be long. Rain would laugh at her daughter's request, and it never was done the way Jocelyn would have liked.

Jocelyn had the prettiest brown eyes, just like her real father, that anyone had ever seen. They weren't too light, but they were just right. When the sun shone on them, it seemed they would change, allowing other colors to have their way on her iris. There were nearly no imperfections as seen in older people with a flurry of veins and dark spots. The whites of her eyes were as the clearest pearl. She was one of the cutest little girls in her small town.

One of the qualities that she inherited from her mother Rain was the way she walked. She had the straightest back in the world, and she always had a big smile on her face that matched the confidence she exuded at such a young age. There wasn't a time that Jocelyn walked with her head down low; it was always held up high with her chin up. Even when she came out of the womb, Jocelyn behaved like she knew the place already and like she came for a reason.

Jocelyn, as she grew up into the intelligent six year old everyone knew she would be, nobody could see the changes that she was about to encounter with the man she loved more than even she knew…her father. It started the day she woke up one Saturday morning, and it was the first time she would put to practice exactly what her poppa Paton wanted her to become.

"Rain, I'm gonna take Jocelyn with me. She say she wanna go, so Junior's out back there," Paton called while lacing up his shoes. In reality, Jocelyn had no idea where her dad was taking her much less did she know that he was even going somewhere. Jocelyn, while Paton spoke to Rain, was sitting out on the front porch drawing in the dirt that she carried over from a pile closer to the trees. She'd spread it out thin enough so that she could practice writing her letters outside with a stick. Paton had been looking at her the whole time while Rain busied herself in the kitchen.

Rain came walking out of the kitchen which was far hotter than the rest of the house because of the stove being on. Sweat dripped from her forehead, and with a kitchen towel, she wiped the top of her head and then pulled her hair back in a ponytail.

"I didn't know you had somewhere to go today, Paton. Where 'bout?" she asked, grabbing a small cup of water that sat on a stool near the wall. The water felt great as it poured inside her mouth and then down her throat. "Thank you, Jesus," she sighed, waiting on him to reply.

"I'm runnin' up round by the store, stop off and get her and Junior some candy…"

"Well, you don't wanna take Junior…"

Paton cut her off before she could even make the suggestion that he predicted. "No, no, Rain." As he answered, he turned around in the chair to look her in her eyes. "A girl needs to spend time alone with her daddy some times," He, then, turned back around. "Me and Junior gonna spend this same time together tomorrow out at the creek. Teach him how to throw a line out, grab some meat. Good time to take him since we runnin' out."

"We are gettin' low. Well, y'all have fun. Bring my baby back in one piece," Rain responded, fanning her face with her straw hat, not thinking anything odd about what she stated until Paton turned back to face her.

He stood tall in his shoes, dark brown jeans and brown shirt and executed a statement that tore through Rain. "She's my baby, too, ain't she?"

Rain's calm and collected demeanor went sour. Her face became deeply stunned to sadness and her attitude stricken with guilt as she felt ashamed about what had been the unspoken truth for such a long time. Without being a bother to him anymore, Rain exited back into the kitchen. Paton watched, without any empathy or remorse for her situation, nor the situation that he was about to place Jocelyn in.

Without a second thought, he stepped outside and looked down at the top of Jocelyn's head where her mom braided all her hair up into a bun that sat directly in the center. Jocelyn didn't even look up at Paton as he walked beside her. She was busy writing her name in short in the dirt – Jocie.

"You ready to go?"

"Where we going, poppa?" she asked, still writing her name over and over again in the dirt, not really paying him much attention.

"I got a surprise for you. Come on here. Get on my back."

She dropped the stick and got so excited that she was going on a piggy back ride with Paton, that she hopped onto his back as soon as he placed his two feet on the bare ground. "Don't let me fall down, Poppa. Momma just did my hair up nice, and she told me if I mess it up, she was gonna be mad. Where we goin'? Can we go to Miss Mary house so I can get me some candy. Everything only cost one penny..."

Paton, although Jocelyn's conversation about her hair and candy would make any other adult smile at the simple thoughts of children, didn't show any emotion while walking forward onto the path that would lead him to Jocelyn's first job. His mind was totally focused on getting her there and treating her for a job well done.

"We on our way to a good friend of mine house. He stay not too far from here, and he gonna get to see all I taught you about being a big girl. I get to show you off...ain't that right?" Paton's words were upbeat, but his expression was blank.

"Yep!" she smiled.

"Got to go get something from him is all. Thought you might like to come with your old poppa." Suddenly, Jocelyn's arms around his neck felt like a rope trying to strangle him to death as he thought about how he killed Haslem. The more Jocelyn wiggled, the more his mind flipped back and forth until a point where he couldn't stand her on his back anymore. Instead of feeling like a child having fun, she felt like a huge weight that he had to carry on his back. "Get down off my shoulders."

"But, poppa..."

"Go on and get down." Paton knelt down to the ground, and Jocelyn grumbled but got down. Before she felt worse, she'd already found something else to do on the way down the wooded trail. She started to kick pine cones. This was always something fun for her to do whenever she was outside. She thought pine cones were the weirdest things because she didn't know why they grew. They looked like the bark of a tree to her in the shape of a flower.

"You wanna race?"

"Race?" she replied with a frown on her face mixed with a smile. "You wanna race...me?" she asked sticking out her neck and pointing at her chest. "Oh, you don't wanna do that 'cause I'm gone win!" Jocelyn took off down the trail, and Paton pretended to chase her until they got to the very end of it. A little ways further, the small hut like house came into view.

"Slow down, Jocie, here's the house right here," he said as he faked his loss of breath to make Jocelyn believe he was really racing. Paton slowed to a walk as he pointed, and Jocelyn ran right up to the door. Before Paton even made it to where Jocelyn was standing, the man opened the door up quickly, staring Paton directly in the face. His eyes were glossed over, and he appeared thirsty and hyper.

Paton walked up closer to Jocelyn who was smiling in the man's face, and then she looked back at Paton, waiting on him to speak. He didn't speak, however. Instead, he nodded to the man and waved Jocelyn on inside.

When Jocelyn walked in, there were some dolls laid out on the floor that she could play with, and immediately, her eyes lit up. Paton had no idea the man he made the deal with would do that, so when Jocelyn ran over to play, the man gave Paton a specific amount of money. From there, he and Paton sat down, talked and drank until Paton felt that Jocelyn was comfortable. That was when Paton told him to exit the room.

Like everything was planned out to the letter, the man got up and went around the corner which lead to the hallway. Paton sat there and flapped the money in his hands. Each time it hit his flesh, he felt proud, like he'd gotten over. As he looked over at Jocelyn, his train of thought made what he was doing with her a fair trade off being that he told the man not to go beyond a certain point.

The innocent Jocelyn turned back around and told her poppa that she was hungry.

"Go on back there and see what he got for you. He got a treat back there, and I got one for you on the way back."

"Yes sir." The poor child got up off the floor and walked around the corner. Fifteen minutes later, she came out a different little girl.

Tears were in her eyes, but her clothes were on her like she'd never taken them off. Her eyes stared hopelessly back into the eyes of the man she knew as her father, but he didn't respond to her gestures that demanded comfort. Instead, he opened the door of the hut while placing a big smile on his face.

"You been a big girl today! Look at you. You done already grown big. Sometimes, the first time is scary, but you'll get used to it. He didn't hurt you, did he?"

Jocelyn didn't answer. She was afraid to make one more sound past the screaming she already did for her poppa to come down the hall and get her. He never came, and she couldn't get loose from the strange man.

The man walked over and gave her a doll and put his hand up to his lips. Paton watched every move the man made while making sure he still had Jocelyn within his mental grasp. Jocelyn took the doll, and then looked back up at him. She then got on his back, and they walked back onto the trail.

"He touched on me, poppa. Why didn't you come get me when I was callin' you?"

"That's what big girls do. All girls do that in order to become women. Your momma not gonna tell you 'bout it because it's supposed to be a secret for life. None of the women you see gonna tell... unless they lose they womanhood."

"I don't wanna do that, poppa."

"Well, clear your eyes up. Keep things quiet, and don't you ever say nothing. I'll bring you some candy after I take you back home. You like your doll?"

"Yes sir."

"Good. I like it, too. I'll teach you some more about things myself soon. Real soon."

"You got you somethin', poppa?" she stated, already seeming to feel better after Paton told her that she would get used to it.

"Yeah, I got everything I need. You just remember to keep your mouth closed tight about everything that just happened."

"I will. I'm a woman now. I am." she stated, resting her chin on his shoulder all the way home. Although her emotions were torn, she felt happy to please her dad in every way because he was always proud of her. Unfortunately, she didn't know that lately, it was all his ploy to exact revenge, and his heart was even more corrupt than it had ever been before. Only now, the corruption relieved itself outdoors instead of remaining contained behind the deep levels of darkness when he closed his eyes to sleep at night in the bedroom.

When they got back home, Rain and Junior weren't there. That was when Paton took her into the bathroom to wash her down regularly to tidy her up for bed. It was his intention to bring happy thoughts into her mind before anyone came to see her face, especially Rain. He knew a mother could tell the slightest difference in a child in less than a second. By the time Rain got back though, Paton already had Jocelyn fed and in the bed while he had more money than he'd had in a long time tucked in his new hiding place that not even Rain knew about.

"Look at my baby," Rain stated sitting next to Jocelyn as she slept after she got back and tucked Junior in the bed. She admired her oldest child while checking her braids and bun that sat on her head to make sure it was still tight and no bugs found their way inside the hair since she watched them go into the woods. "He brought you back to me. He brought you back to me…and you look just fine," she sighed a whisper. She then reached over and tucked her new doll baby closer to her before leaving the room. When she turned the corner, Paton was there waiting for her.

"I got you somethin'," he stated as he leaned against the wall.

Startled, she responded, "What's that?"

From behind his back, he revealed a handful of roses, and the sight of them made her smile. Paton had already planned on disguising his evil with some good to distract Rain from thinking about whatever happened that day. He didn't want to be questioned, so his act of being so in love with her was the best there was. He'd become a master at deception having had been deceived so well by her himself.

She moved toward him, and received her precious gift. Then, he took her by the hand, and she was grateful that he did so for all the pain that she'd put him through. Finally, they ended the night, Rain overwhelmed with guilt and Paton overtaken with deceit and evil.

After Paton and Rain made love, when Rain fell into a deep sleep, Paton got up from his bed, grabbed a bottle of liquor and his clothes and left the house. He walked for a long way off, beyond the creek until he finally made it back behind the house of the late Haslem.

He sat in the high grass and drank himself into a stupor as he watched images of himself killing Haslem all over again. Bending his fingers as if he had Haslem's neck in his grip again, he pictured the man dying until he fell lifeless. On his right side he started to hallucinate, seeing his deceased father come walking toward him while his mother walked away from him on his left side. When he stood up and tried to run for her, she only started to walk faster until he heard a voice in his ear…

"Stop whining, boy! Don't let nobody break you."

When he looked to the side, he saw his dad's eyes and they were ice cold staring back at him. Paton grabbed his head and tried not to listen, but when he closed his eyes and opened them again, there was his dad staring him in the face. The deceased John Lee then moved from Paton's vision, and that was when Paton laid eyes on Jocelyn sitting on the ground in the dark grass. She was making a doll out of the strands. Paton started walking toward her, but before he made it there, she turned to face him. The look on her face was engrained in sadness. Then, she stood up and walked toward Paton, and when she got within three feet from him, Paton bent down to meet her. That was when Jocelyn handed him the grass doll she made, and as he grabbed for it, she snatched it back, startling Paton. Finally, she turned toward the house of Haslem causing him to turn to look at it, too, but when he turned back to face her, he met the worst thing ever in his sight. She was smirking, and for the first time, sound came from her mouth…

"That there is my real daddy."

Paton raised his hand, and with all his strength, tried to smack her down to the ground, but it was him who hit the ground as Jocelyn faded away, her smile being that last thing to go. Frantically, Paton reached inside his pocket and pulled out a match. Then, he ran back to his bottle of alcohol which was hidden in a lower patch of grass. Haslem's house stood firm on the ground like nothing had ever happened, so just like Paton did when he was a boy, he walked over to it and set the house on fire. He watched it burn from afar.

The curse that Haslem had over Paton's life never faded while he continuously hated Jocelyn in the worst ways imaginable, passing her from man to man, stripping her of all her innocence.

THE END

This was the third and final book in The Secret Novel Collection.

MORE AKIRIM PRESS BOOKS

Books by Mirika Mayo Cornelius

Secret

Colored Lily: Poppa Took My Innocence

Paton

Ain't Quite What I Thought!

Ain't Quite What I Thought! 2

First Degree Sins

Inside the Gates of Doons

Sunny Sides of My Shade

Murders at Gabriel's Trails: The Complete 5 Part Series plus bonus Sins of Bain

Sins of Bain

Deception at Gabriel's Trails: The Complete Series

Curse the Cotton

Disguised by a Raging Smile

Most Wanted Felon

Books by Rod Cornelius

Ugly

Single Again

Diggin' Gold

The Trusted

Ghetto Eyes

The Best Kept Secrets

Whatever It Takes

<u>Books by Cyan Deane</u>

Dead Man's Mayhem

Execution's Karma

Preview CURSE THE COTTON
by Mirika Mayo Cornelius

"Stop right here! Stop right here now or I swear 'fore the Lord and your daddy I'll whip you myself, Cosah!" Her chest rose up and sunk down rapidly as she felt the blood rush to her head, nearly causing her to faint. She hadn't eaten anything all night long after picking cotton, and she was just about to when Cosah woke up, not even speaking, to head out to the cotton fields as he did every morning. It was obvious that he was still not feeling well, but he'd been raised to tolerate just about anything. Therefore, angry and sick, he tried to escape even looking at his mother but was forced to halt when she raised her voice, something that she never did.

Cosah stood there. He stared at the vast cotton fields that shown nothing but white underneath the rising sun. His six year old body just stood there with a big rip in his dusty, white shirt and worn down pants that were far too short in length while his toes curled in the shoes he wore because they were too small, all while his back remained turned to his mother as the tears rolled down his face. He continued to look at the cotton, like the cotton was all he was going to end up doing in his whole life...until he died like his father.

Shelone thought about walking toward him as her heart deceived her with pain for her child, the child that she knew she had to raise to be strong and almost careless to make it in the world. Although that emotion tugged at her to run and save him, she ignored it and demanded his respect instead, no matter how much she understood how he felt. There was too much at stake for her to allow him to disobey or dishonor her at any time.

"Walk back here right now, Cosah," she calmly stated, forcing back her sadness in order to portray strength. Cosah slowly turned around to face the only mother that he'd ever known in his short lifetime, and that was a blessing in itself. Then, he began to walk back, his head held high, however, she could tell his soul was aching. When he reached her, she began to speak again, but was stopped by his voice.

"I ain't never gonna see my daddy again, Mama," he cried, his little chest swelling up as much as it could before it finally forced the pain out in a collapsing wail. "He wasn't supposed to die, Mama, he wasn't supposed to go nowhere! He said we was gonna stop pickin' and be free," he drowned in his sorrow, grabbing onto his mother's dress like it was his lifeline to a peaceful heaven.

When his words entered his mother's ears about freedom, she squeezed him tightly, shaken with fear and grief simultaneously as her tears began to puddle on top of his thick, dark brown hair that reminded her of his father. She didn't know Marcus talked to him about freedom and escape. She knew they had their talks, but she had no idea that the root of freedom had already been sown into Cosah's heart so early. She knew what the thought of freedom came with if the internal had no control over how much it screamed. If it screamed too loudly, the whites would hear it, and they would destroy it.

"Cosah," she stammered, still flustered with his words, but he interrupted.

"What happened to him...tell me," he cried.

Shelone's strength completely left her body and she collapsed onto the floor with him, rocking her son back and forth. Then, finally she told him everything, how the whites ran him off over a crime he had nothing to do with. "And you know your daddy. He wasn't gonna let nobody take him without a fight, but he knew he couldn't beat all those whites. He had to run. And he could run fast, just like you, baby. He just couldn't swim really good." She took a deep breath. "Instead of him turning and watching death catch up to him, he swam the best he could. The slave they took to help the hunt said he saw him go down in the water. He didn't holler for the whites while he was looking at your father go down. He said that your daddy chose to die in the water because he hollered out the words "I'm free!". Then he let the water take him. By that time, the whites ran up to the slave that saw everything, and he told them what happened. They forced that slave in the water to find him, made him stay out there a good long bit, but he told me that when he saw your daddy's body in the water, he didn't pull it up. Instead, he pushed him on down further…said he did it so that your father could keep his freedom. Them whites would have drug him out and laid him here for all us to see. Cosah," she cried softly, "your daddy did right. As long as he was living, he wasn't gonna let fear of death or whites keep you from dreaming, so he died. Died right there…and I know it's so you and your sisters wouldn't see." She pulled his head up and looked him in his watery eyes. "You hold in the freedom until it's able to come out, and when it can come out, that's when you run. That's when we are all gonna run, Cosah. We gonna be free. Wipe your eyes," she continued, wiping the tears from her own cheeks. Then, she pulled herself and her child together. "I owe you that, and we will get it. Hold it here," she said, placing her hand on his heart. "Keep your mouth closed…until I say so. Don't show your pain."

Cosah remained near his mother for longer than usual that morning so that he could calm down. His sisters were already out in the fields, and it was only five minutes later that he was able to go out along with them. Before he left, he stopped at the cabin door and turned back to face his mother.

"He better not sleep, Mama."

She turned around with Abraham on her breast, rocking him so as to soothe him during feeding time. "What you say, Cosah?"

"I'm gonna kill Mr. Marksman…one day."

Preview UGLY by Rod Cornelius

He stood in front of the mirror with his head hanging down as he hovered over the bathroom sink with both arms stretched out against the wall. He had been positioned that way for a little bit over a half hour. He was fully dressed in his usual attire–black hoodie, baggie blue jeans and boots. It was another first day and another new school with a brand new group of potential tormentors. Julius had been dreading this day for months–three to be exact–ever since the day him, his mother, and his good for nothing stepfather moved into this new place.

Although his mom provided her best efforts to talk up the new school, there was no hiding the fact that Washington High was known for being one of the worst schools in the entire district, and possibly the whole state. But the rent here was good and his mother was hopeful that this school would be different for him than all the rest.

The neighbors told her many positive changes had come to the troubled institution near the end of the previous school year resulting from the successful basketball program there. They also told her that the school board had brought in a mostly new staff and a hardnosed veteran principal that didn't take any shit and that he was calling all the shots.

It made Julius no difference because he didn't play any sports, and he did his best to stay out of people's way, more specifically school staff. This was his senior year, and as with every school year, he was determined to do what he had to do to make it go by as quickly and as smoothly as possible. Of course, with his looks, he often found that task extremely difficult to accomplish.

He slowly lifted his head and gazed into the mirror. He had hoped when his eyes returned to the reflection in that spotty old bathroom mirror another face would appear. A handsome face. A likeable face. Any face but his.

Big nose, huge lips, jet black skin and a bumpy forehead. He knew he was stuck with three out of four of those features for life, but even a complete surrender on drinking sodas and eating sweets did nothing to smoothen out his rough skin.

He swiped a towel hanging from the shower rack and began dampening it. He gently applied the cloth to his face and then began to violently scrub his face with it. His intention was to wipe his face completely off of his head, but he was unsuccessful again. He tossed the towel across the shower rack and sorrowfully stared at himself in the mirror once more. *Why me?*